MW00781315

The Last Ride

Gregory Payette

8 Flags Publishing, Inc.

This one's for Mom and Dad

Sign up for the newsletter on my website:

GregoryPayette.com

Once or twice a month I'll send you updates and news. Plus, you'll be the first to hear about new releases with special prices. If you'd like to receive the Henry Walsh prequel (for free) use the sign-up form here: **GregoryPayette.com/crossroad**

Chapter 1

BARRINGTON'S WAS A RESTAURANT for people fancier than I was, or the type who liked to believe they were perhaps something special. If you happened to enjoy eighteen-dollar cocktails and large plates with barely enough food to fill a space between your teeth, then Barrington's was for you.

Angela Thompson appeared to be looking my way when I walked past the tall plants and a fish tank, separating the bar from the restaurant's foyer. She gave me a nod and raised her martini glass, taking a sip without taking her eyes off me.

Angela might've been a little older than she'd been in the photo I saw of her, but she was an attractive woman, although the dim lights over the bar made it hard to get a good enough look.

She watched and smiled, extending her hand to shake mine. "You must be Henry."

GREGORY PAYETTE

"Sorry I'm late," I said, looking around the bar. I felt like everyone had turned to look at me. But it always felt that way when I walked up to a bar I'd never been in before.

I gazed around at the well-dressed crowd, filling most of the seats around the long, U-shaped bar. It was twice the size of any bar I'd normally spend my time at, including the one at my friend Billy's restaurant. The men at Barrington's all wore ties, although loose around their necks. I guess I'd describe the women—including Angela—to be dressed professionally. I couldn't think of any other way to describe it.

I looked at my Sperry Top-Siders, feeling a little underdressed with my short-sleeved shirt. At least it had buttons.

Angela looked at her watch and turned it on her wrist. "You're right on time."

A glass, half full with gold-colored liquor was on the bar in front of the empty stool next to Angela. "Is someone sitting here?"

Before she could answer, a man's hand reached from behind and grabbed the glass. "Excuse me," he said.

It was an older gentleman, maybe the only other person at the bar besides me who didn't dress like he'd come from a corporate board meeting.

I stepped out of his way. "I'm sorry, I—"

"No, please. Go ahead." He put his warm, heavy hand on my back and grabbed the glass. "I'm leaving."

Angela put her hand on my arm. "Go ahead. Sit down. He's been 'leaving' for an hour now. If you don't take his seat, he'll

2

never go home." She winked at Roy, sipping her martini with a somewhat mischievous smile.

The man reached out for my hand. "Roy Mason," he said, squeezing my hand hard. He held it a bit too long, like he wanted to wait for me to cry mercy.

Angela told him who I was before I had a chance to.

Roy finally let go of my hand. "The private investigator, huh?"

"Roy is a friend of John's," Angela said.

I slid onto the stool and faced him.

"John and I were more than just friends," Roy said. "Two peas in a pod."

"I'm sorry about your loss," I said, then glanced at Angela. "To both of you."

Roy shook his head, looking toward the floor. "Sometimes a freak accident is all it takes, end a good man's life."

Angela leaned toward me. "Roy seems to think I'm wasting your time. He's got a lot of friends at the sheriff's office and refuses to believe they would *ever* make a mistake. But I don't think it hurts anyone to make sure we know the truth, does it?"

Roy finished what was in his glass and placed it on the bar. "Okay, I'm leaving. For real this time." He gave me a quick nod. "Good meeting you." He kissed Angela on the back of her head. "We'll catch up later, hon."

She gave him a half-hearted wave over her shoulder but didn't turn from the bar. "Bye now, Roy."

I watched him limp, going past the tall plants and the fish tank, and out the door.

Angela said, "Like I told you on the phone, I'm on an island, all alone with this. Nobody wants to believe something else could've happened to John. It's like they all just want to put it away and ignore the facts because the sheriff's office said it was an accident." Angela waved the bartender over. "Kyle? Would you please come over here and get my friend a drink?" She tapped the top of her glass. "I could use a refill myself."

The bartender walked toward us, wiping his hands on the towel draped over his shoulder. "What would you like?"

"Jack Daniels." I put two fingers in the air. "Two ice cubes."

He walked away, and I said to Angela, "Do you want to tell me more about what happened to Mr. Thompson?"

Angela peered into her glass. "Aren't you going to ask me why the ex-wife is hiring a private investigator?"

"Bob told me you were in business together," I said. "So I assumed—"

"John and I were business partners. But we were more than that. I don't mean we were lovers. Not anymore. It started, we were just two kids out of college who were in the right place at the right time and started a business together. We were lucky."

"You met in college?"

Angela nodded.

I said, "And John was married to someone else?"

"The last one, his widow; she was wife number three."

Kyle walked over and put a martini down in front of Angela and put a glass down in front of me that was filled to the top with ice.

Angela pointed at my glass. "Didn't you ask for two ice cubes?"

I took a sip. "That's all right."

Angela waved for Kyle and said to me, "It shouldn't be that difficult to follow a simple request, should it?"

"Really, it's not a big deal," I said. "I don't like it watered down."

Kyle walked over. "Is everything all right?"

"Yeah, good," I said.

But Angela wasn't having it. "Kyle," she said, grabbing the glass from my hand. She slid it toward Kyle. "Would you mind giving Henry what he'd asked for?"

Kyle said, "That's a Jack Daniels. Isn't that what he wanted?"

Angela shook her head. "He specifically said he wanted two cubes of ice. Does that look like two cubes of ice? Four minutes from now, it'll be a Jack and water."

I gave Kyle a look like I had nothing to do with it.

He dumped what was in my glass and filled it again from the bottle, placing two cubes in it with the metal scoop. "Sorry about that," he said, and turned away.

Angela sipped her martini, holding the glass by the stem. She said, "You want something a certain way, you ask for it. You don't get it, you demand it." She gave me a questioning look. "You're not a pushover, are you?"

I cracked a grin and shook my head. "I like to pick my battles," I said.

Angela turned toward me on the stool, her skirt hiked halfway up her thighs and her knee rubbing against mine. "I don't know how much you know," she said, "other than what I told you on the phone. But I might as well start from the beginning." Angela sipped her martini and picked an olive from the glass, popping it in her mouth. "John was what you might consider an avid biker. He rode two, three times a week. And he never missed his Sunday morning rides. It was his favorite day. No matter what—rain or shine—John would be out there at seven o'clock in the morning."

"Did he always ride at Losco Park?" I said.

"He did. He liked the dirt trails there." She got Kyle's attention, pointing to the glass.

"So, what happened?" I said.

"Well, as far as I understand, John got up like he did every Sunday morning for his bike ride. I guess, for the last time." She paused. "Two boys found him on the edge of a pond. The sheriff's office claims he went off the trail and down the side of a hill. They believe he must've been out of control, hitting his head before his bike slid into the pond. They found him facedown in four inches of water."

"But from what I've looked into, his death wasn't caused by drowning," I said.

"Head injuries. I don't know if you're familiar with Losco Park, but there are trees and boulders all around that pond. They say he likely hit his head more than once." She picked an olive from her empty glass and bit half of it. "Sounds a bit odd, if you ask me."

I straightened in my seat, moving my leg away from her knee rubbing against me. "You said you went over there? To Losco Park, where it happened?"

"Roy took me," she said. "I wanted to—"

Kyle put another drink in front of me and walked away.

Angela tapped the side of her martini glass with her long, red-painted fingernails. "Here's what I don't get: John wore that helmet every time he rode his bike. I mean, we're in the insurance business. We're all about minimizing risk." She picked up her martini and held it in front of her chin, staring straight ahead like she was thinking.

"Angela?"

She paused before she spoke. "John would've worn that helmet to bed if it didn't mess with his sex life."

"But they found his helmet," I said. "Near the trail."

I waited for a response, but there wasn't one. "If that's all there is, that you believe he would have normally worn his helmet, then..." I stopped myself. I didn't want to insult my new and only client. "Is there anything else? Something more that—"

"Isn't that what I'm hiring you to do?"

Chapter 2

IT WAS LATE MORNING when I met Alex at the bar at Billy's Place. Alex Jepson had worked with me as the assistant director of security for the Jacksonville Sharks baseball team, although took over as director when I left to start Walsh Investigations.

For Alex, the off-season had begun, since the Sharks never made it past the regular season. It was good news for her as it was for me when I worked there, because vacation started earlier than it had for the other clubs that actually made it to the playoffs once in a while.

She faced me from the laptop opened in front of her on the bar.

"I guess you got my message?" I said.

She sipped from a cup of tea and placed it down before answering. "I was reading up on it. And from what I can find, I don't see how his death was anything more than an accident. He went down a steep hill and hit his head. It's not like bike accidents are uncommon," she said.

"But where are you looking? If you're reading from the local media, they're being fed whatever the sheriff's office tells them," I said.

She gave me a look like she didn't appreciate my skepticism.

My good friend and owner of Billy's Place, Billy Wu, was behind the bar, as he was most of the time. He walked out through the swinging door from the kitchen and came over to me and Alex. "New client, huh?"

I said, "Fell in my lap."

"Those are the best ones," Billy said. "Alex said it's John Thompson's ex-wife?"

"You know him?" I said.

Billy shook his head. "Not well, but I know he's a bigwig insurance man around here. He used to run those commercials late at night."

"I met with her last night," I said. "The ex."

He said, "She thinks he was murdered?"

"Well, she didn't say murdered. But she's not convinced it was an accident."

Alex said, "I know you think all I did was read some new articles online, but I actually spoke to Mike, to see what he could tell me."

I laughed. "Yeah, detectives love when private investigators are hired to prove them wrong."

"I'm sure he doesn't like the idea of you being on his back again," Billy said, wiping a liquor bottle, a crooked grin on his face. He walked away and put the bottle on the shelf at the back of the bar.

"I didn't give him any specifics or even mention your name," Alex said. "I tried to pick his brain, made it like I was curious about it."

I said, "So what'd he say?"

"Exactly what it said online. Investigation's already wrapped up. No foul play."

I reached for a cup of coffee Billy slid in front of me. I took a sip and said to Alex, "Was it Mike's case?"

"No, but he said he heard about Angela Thompson. He said she was being very demanding, requesting they keep the investigation open. But then she stopped bothering them."

I reached for a menu and skimmed over the sandwiches.

Alex said, "So what else did she say?"

"Mrs. Thompson? Just like I said on the message, she said he normally would have worn his helmet."

"There's got to be something else," she said.

"Of course," I said. "But do you want to know what she told me when I said that to her? She said it was *my* job to figure it out... that's why she hired a private investigator." I sipped my coffee. "I'm meeting her later today, at her office. Do you think you'll be able to come with me?"

"I'd love to," she said. "And, so you know, there are rumors floating around that Bob might be looking to sell the team."

"Yeah? You think it's true?" I said.

"If they are, it means I could be out of work. So I might as well get my feet wet now. Like I told you in the beginning, I'll do whatever I can to help you. But keep in mind I might be looking for a job if Bob does decide to sell."

"I don't know how often I'll have something like this land in my lap. But so far, based on the calls I've been getting, there are plenty of unfaithful spouses out there. Although I'm not sure I want to spend my days watching someone cheat on their wife."

"Women cheat too," Alex said.

I smiled, nodding. "I know. I meant... I mean, if this works out, it'll be good for business. And I won't be able to do it alone."

· · · ● ·● · ● · ● · ·

Alex and I walked into the lobby of a high-rise office building off Riverside Avenue, east of the river, and were met by a heavyset security guard eating his lunch behind a desk. He didn't move or look up when we first walked in through the revolving door, but raised his eyes, chewing whatever food he'd stuffed in his mouth. He spoke out of one side of his mouth. "Can I help you?"

"Thompson Insurance?" I said, even though I didn't need the man's help figuring out where to go.

He swallowed, like he swallowed his entire mouthful in one go, and tapped on a clipboard on the desk. "Sign here."

11

I signed my name, and he said, "I need both signatures." He held his gaze on Alex and pushed himself up from his chair, lifting his baggy brown pants by his belt. Alex signed, and he said, "Straight down the hall, turn right and take the elevator to the twelfth floor."

We found our way to the elevator and rode it up, arriving a few steps from the front entrance to Thompson Insurance.

We walked through the double glass doors and to the unoccupied reception desk. It was quiet, and almost appeared as if the office was deserted.

"You sure she knows you're coming?" Alex said.

Before I answered, a tall, attractive woman with red hair, dressed businesslike, walked through the door. She came straight toward me, arm extended. Shaking my hand, she said, "I'm Kayla Morton."

"Henry Walsh," I said. "This is Alex Jepson."

She shook Alex's hand and turned for the door she'd just walked through. "Follow me."

We did as she said and were led into a conference room with a dark wood table as long as my boat. There were twelve matching leather chairs on either side and one on each end. A large flat-screen TV hung on the wall on the far end of the table with a wall of shelves filled with books on the other. I wondered if the books were just for show.

Kayla said, "Angela's running a little late. But she'll be with you shortly. Eric will be here any minute."

"Eric?" I said.

"Oh, maybe Angela didn't mention him. It's John's brother. I thought maybe you knew he'd be in the meeting."

I sat in one of the chairs at the far end. "Does he work here?"

Alex sat next to me.

Kayla nodded, pulling at a strand of her hair. "Angela thought it would be a good idea if Eric was here. He's a little, well... I'll let you judge for yourself." She reached for the door. "I'll let Angela know you're here." She started to leave but stopped, turning back to me and Alex. "Can I get either of you a drink?"

Alex and I both shook our heads, and Kayla left the room.

A moment later, a man I guessed was somewhere in his early thirties, stepped into the conference room, his shirt untucked and pants wrinkled. He didn't appear to care much for a razor. Not that I blamed him.

He had his head down toward his phone, without a word, walking toward the seat at the far end of the table from where Alex and I sat. I watched him, still preoccupied with his phone, thumbs moving rapidly on the screen. After a handful of seconds he finally put his device on the table. "You must be the detectives?"

I gave Alex a quick glance out of the corner of my eye and said, "I'm Henry Walsh. This is Alex Jepson."

"You're not one of ours?" Eric said.

"One of your *what*?"

"Investigators? We have a handful who work for us, mostly to investigate fraud and such, so I thought—"

"No, we're not one of your investigators. My firm... my, uh, agency is called Walsh Investigations."

I wasn't sure I came out like a bumbling fool or not. But the truth was the business was brand new. I didn't even know the right way to refer to it. Was it an agency? A firm? I wanted it to appear like it was a bigger operation than it was. But I realized I probably needed to tighten up my pitch, although the reality was that I was nothing more than a solo private investigator. The ink on my license was barely dry, and what little experience I had under my belt, other than solving Sharks' third baseman Lance Moreau's murder, was one of the few times I'd followed a cheating spouse.

Eric appeared a bit perplexed. He pulled at his chin. "Now, why would Angela bring someone else in when we already..." Eric picked up his phone before he finished and began tapping away with his thumbs.

The glass door opened, and Kayla walked into the room, her eyes on Eric. "You're here?"

Eric glanced up from his phone. "Always so perceptive, Kayla." He let a slight snort out his nose and went back to tapping on his phone.

Kayla stared back at him, her nostrils almost flared. She pulled at a strand of her long, red hair, twisting it around her finger. "Henry, Alex. I'm so sorry. Angela's going to have to reschedule your meeting for later."

Eric jumped up from his seat. "What a shame." He walked out of the room without a word.

I waited for the door to close and said to Kayla, "Is he always like that?"

She said, "He doesn't understand why Angela wants to have someone investigate his brother's death."

"Oh." I got up from the chair. "Should we wait in the reception area, or—"

"No, she's on a call. It's with one of our bigger clients. There's some sort of issue, and these calls can sometimes go on for hours."

Chapter 3

I reached over the rail of the boat and pulled down the two folding lawn chairs I had taken from my parents' house after they moved from our home—the one I grew up in—in Fernandina Beach. They were the old-school aluminum chairs that folded, with the green mesh strips. I remembered my parents bringing them to the beach when I was young.

An orange glow from the lamps along the docks and over the marina parking lot reflected off the St. Johns River. A cool breeze carried the welcome fall air toward us.

I set both chairs down on the dock, facing the river, then climbed back onto the boat and got Alex a sweatshirt, then headed down to the galley for the six-pack of Corona I had in the fridge.

Alex was already in one of the chairs on the dock, her feet stretched in front of her, looking out toward the river. She had her arms folded, wearing nothing but short sleeves. "Here you go," I said, giving her the sweatshirt. "Temperature's dropped a bit."

"Oh, I'm all right," she said. "You didn't have to—"

"Don't worry, it's clean," I said.

She laughed, and pulled the sweatshirt over her head.

I handed her the open bottle of Corona.

"No Jack?" she said.

I took a drink from my bottle and sat in the chair. "Not tonight."

The boat I lived on was docked at a place called Trout River Marina. It was not, technically, my boat, although I was lucky enough to be the official caretaker while the owner—a friend of mine—had been living in Australia. He'd gone down for business but decided he wasn't coming back. At least not anytime soon. So I was lucky enough to be the beneficiary. I needed a place to live, and he needed someone to take care of his boat until, and if, he ever came back.

I glanced at my watch. "It's almost nine," I said. "I never heard from Angela."

Alex stood from her chair and leaned against the boat, facing me. "Who is this friend you mentioned, the man you met at Barrington's?"

"You mean Angela's friend?"

Alex nodded, sipping her beer.

I said, "Roy Mason. I don't know much about him, other than she introduced him as John's good friend. But the way they acted with each other, it was almost as if they had something going on between them."

"Do you mean, romantically?"

"Hard to say. But he didn't seem to believe she needed to hire a private investigator. He said he trusts that the sheriff's office knows what they're doing."

"I'd agree with that," Alex said.

"But they're also human," I said. "They make mistakes, like anyone else."

"Did she mention anything else about him? Or why he wouldn't be interested in at least finding out whether or not something else could've happened to his friend?"

"We didn't get into it," I said. "But that's why we need to meet with her. And I'd like to talk to him myself again. Sooner than later."

I heard my phone ring and realized I'd left it up on the boat. I jumped from my chair and hurried up onto the deck. I followed the ringer and spotted it on one of the bench cushions. It was Angela calling. But by the time I answered, she'd hung up.

I dialed her right back, and she answered on a half ring. "Henry? I'm glad you called right back. I'm sorry about what happened earlier. I had a client emergency. It really turned into quite the mess, and I spent the evening putting out a few fires. I hope I didn't waste your time."

"It's not a big deal," I said. "I was lucky enough to meet John's charming brother."

"Oh. I'm sorry about that. I told him to join us, only because I thought he had the right to know what's going on. He and John weren't even that close, but he's his brother. He certainly takes some getting used to."

I said, "So everything's all set with your client's emergency?"

"I believe it is. In fact, you met him last night at Barrington's. Roy Mason."

Alex leaned on the rail and watched me come down off the boat.

I said, "Roy Mason's one of your clients?"

"Not just any client. He's our *biggest* client. I'm surprised he didn't mention it when you two met. It's usually one of the first things he says when I introduce him. Roy wants everyone to know he's not some small fish." The other line went quiet. "The truth is if it wasn't for Roy, Thompson Insurance wouldn't be what it is today."

"What kind of business is he in?" I said.

Angela let out a quick laugh. "What kind of business *isn't* he in..." She paused. "Real estate. Construction... even the restaurant industry."

"Do you think he'd be willing to talk to me?" I said. "I'm going to have to talk to him. I hope there won't be any friction, considering he doesn't sound like he's very receptive to having me involved in this investigation."

Angela went quiet for a moment. "Well, I'd like to think he would. But he even brought it up on our call, that he thinks I'm wasting money hiring you."

"I'm not sure that means he won't talk to me," I said.

"Well, you're the expert. I'll leave it up to you."

Alex was seated in the lawn chair, listening but looking out into the darkness over the river.

I thought for a moment. "Angela, I need to ask you something. I hope you don't take it the wrong way... and I know you said you want me to do the digging... but are you being straight with me? Is there something else besides the fact John didn't wear a helmet that's making you suspicious of his death?"

I heard her sigh into the phone.

"Listen," she said. "If there was something else, I'd tell you." She was quiet for a few seconds. "Would you call me crazy if I told you it's a feeling I have in my gut?"

"I've been known to make a few moves myself over the years, strictly based on the feeling I have in my gut. So, no, I wouldn't call you crazy. But we are going to need something more. At least, eventually."

"And, as I told you when we met, that's what I've hired you to do. It's up to you to find that evidence, isn't it?"

I thought about it for a moment. "Can we meet in the morning? I'd really like to ask you a few more questions."

"I'm sorry, but I'm heading up to Atlanta for the day. I'll be back in the late afternoon or perhaps early evening." She was quiet. "If you don't mind, you can meet me at my house once I return?"

"I'll have to check with Alex, make sure I—"

"I thought maybe it'd be okay if you came alone? I'd feel more comfortable that way. To have both of you there... I don't know. I'd feel like I'm getting ganged up on."

"That wouldn't be the case," I said. "Alex is very good at—"

"I'd like you to come alone, all right? Am I asking for too much? Because it's really just a simple request from your client."

I felt a lump in my throat. I was getting the feeling Angela was the pushy kind of client I normally wasn't looking for. Although, maybe pushy was too strong of a word. I said, "What time would you like me there?"

"I'll be home by seven, at the latest. Anytime after that. Do you know where my house is, in San Marco?"

"I know where it is. I'll be there at seven. And in the meantime, if you're okay with it, I'd like to talk to Roy again while you're up in Atlanta?"

"Sure, you can talk to Roy. But what about John's widow? You might want to talk to her, too."

"She's on my list," I said. "I assume she already knows about me?"

Angela took a moment before she answered. "I haven't told her anything about it."

"You're telling me Michelle Thompson doesn't know you've hired someone to investigate her husband's death?"

"I'm sorry. Is that a problem?" Angela said. "I haven't gotten around to calling her. I'm sure she'll understand, once you let her know."

Chapter 4

I DROVE OUT TO Deerwood where John Thompson's widow lived alone in a five-thousand-square-foot brick home with six bedrooms and five baths. Hopefully, with one less person in the house, she'd finally have enough space.

Before I made it into the Thompson's neighborhood, I had to stop at the gated entrance. A guard stepped out of a small brick building, with sunglasses over his eyes, and approached my car. He held a clipboard in his hand and walked around toward the rear of my car. I watched him in the rearview as he looked at my license plate, appearing to write down the number. He walked over and stood outside my window. "Who're you here to see?"

"Michelle Thompson," I said. "She lives at—"

"I know where Mrs. Thompson lives." He flipped a sheet of paper on his clipboard. "State your name, please."

"Henry Walsh."

He ran his finger down the paper. "Is she expecting you?"

"Well, no. Not exactly."

He looked over the top of his sunglasses. "Not exactly?" Clearing his throat, he said, "Well then, I'm sorry, but I can't let you in if your name's not on the list."

His name was on a name tag, pinned to his chest. "Oh, uh, well... Mickey, wouldn't it be an option to call her? Ask if she'll see me?"

He fixed his glasses over his eyes, nodding. "Sure, I can call her, but maybe you should go ahead and first tell me why you're here, so I can relay that information to Mrs. Thompson. I don't know how well you know her or if you're some kind of friend of hers, but she's had a very difficult tragedy she's dealing with right now, and—"

"That's why I'm here. I'm actually... I'm a private investigator. I'm here to talk to her about Mr. Thompson."

"A private investigator?" He pulled at his chin. "Do you have some kind of identification?"

I nodded and took my laminated license from my pocket and handed it to him.

He looked it over. "Florida State Private Investigator, huh? So what is it, exactly, that you're investigating?"

"John Thompson's death. If you'd just give her a quick call? You can tell her Angela Thompson sent me."

Mickey kept his gaze on me for a moment. "Mr. Thompson's ex-wife sent you?"

I nodded, and he walked back inside the brick building, closing the door behind him.

I watched the building until the door finally opened a couple of minutes later. Mickey stepped out and waved for me to drive forward, then pointed straight through the gate that had started to open. "You know where the house is?"

"No, I—"

"Number Seventy-One Eighty-Six Summer Ridge Drive. Go straight through the gate and take the first right. Take the second left. Go down the far end of Summer Ridge Drive until you see the two-story brick home right after the bridge over the creek running alongside the property."

• • • ● • ● • ● • •

I pulled in the driveway off Summer Ridge Drive and pulled in behind a white BMW parked in the shade in front of one of the garage doors. A small sticker on the vehicle's back window said Deerwood Country Club.

The irrigation system was running, spraying water onto most of the brick walkway leading to the brick steps at the front door. I tried to time it so I wouldn't get sprayed, jumping over the puddles formed on the walkway.

I rang the doorbell and waited, listening for someone on the other side of the door. At first nobody answered. I knocked as the door opened. A short woman, fairly attractive and a bit on the heavy side, stood in the doorway. She was much younger than I'd expected a woman to be, married to a sixty-year-old man.

She put a smile on her face, although I got the feeling it was a bit forced. "You're the private investigator Mickey called about?"

I nodded and reached out to shake her hand. "Henry Walsh."

"Michelle," she said. "Mickey said Angela sent you?"

"She did."

She stepped back from the door and welcomed me in.

The house was even bigger than it appeared from the outside. And it was much cooler. Almost cold, with the air-conditioner seemingly on full blast. The foyer we stood in was high, long, and wide enough that you could fit a couple of basketball hoops and have a full-court game.

I followed Michelle down a hallway.

She said, "I wish Angela had called to tell me about you." She continued into a kitchen and stepped around a large granite-top island. "I guess I'm not surprised Angela would hire you without even talking to me about it first."

The tone of her voice had me thinking perhaps the two didn't get along.

Michelle walked across the large, open kitchen. "With there being a wife between me and Angela, you wouldn't think there'd be so much hostility."

"Hostility? Angela didn't mention anything about—"

"I always felt it was the age thing. She never understood why John would want to marry a younger woman. But he used to tell me not to take it personally." She pulled out a glass pitcher from the refrigerator. "Would you like some iced tea?"

I stood leaning against the island. "Sure."

She poured two glasses and placed one in front of me. "Now, Angela and John's second wife, I can understand why *they* never got along."

"Oh, I guess I understand what you mean," I said.

She took a drink of her iced tea and made an exaggerated "Mmmmm," holding the glass in front of her, looking at it from the side. "That's good tea, isn't it?"

I hadn't taken a sip but went ahead and did so. I nodded. "It's good."

"I don't know how much you know about Angela or his second wife, Theresa. But the two were actually friends before John and Theresa"—she looked into her glass, then broke out a big smile, staring back at me with her eyes wide—"*when* John and Theresa got together."

"Did you know Angela before you married John?"

She shook her head. "No. I've never really gotten to know her very well. John never liked the idea of me being around her. I'd never even been to his office. And the one time he invited her here, when we hosted a party, Angela didn't show up."

"Wait," I said. "Did you say you've *never* been to John's office?"

She nodded, staring back at me.

I took another sip of the iced tea.

"You like that, huh? My granddaddy taught me how to make it, told me the key is to let it soak up the hot Florida sun for three-to-four hours. It really does make a difference." She had a look on her face like a thought entered her head. "Oh no!" She ran to the oven, slipped on an oven mitt and opened the door, removing a sheet of cookies. "This is my nana's cookie recipe." She placed the hot sheet pan on top of the stove. "As soon as they cool down, you can try a few. Take some home with you."

Michelle looked up at a clock hung high on the wall. "Oh, shoot. I'm sorry, but I have to leave. I have a tennis match I have to go to."

I put my glass down on top of the island. "Would you mind if we continue this again later? I'd really like to ask you a few questions."

"Well, I guess if you can call me first, it'll be easier than showing up like you did." She pulled a piece of paper out of a drawer, wrote something on it, and handed it to me. "Here's my number." She walked back to one of the cabinets near the stove, pulled down a plastic container, then filled it with cookies. "Here," she said, handing me the container. "Be careful, they're still very hot."

"Thank you. If it's all right, I'll call you later this afternoon?"

She walked ahead of me, down the hall, toward the front of the house. She stood in the foyer and opened the front door, waiting for me to leave. "It was very nice to meet you, Mr. Walsh."

"You can call me Henry," I said, walking past her and out the door. I turned on the top step. "You didn't say... do you know John's second wife? I didn't have a chance to ask Angela about her, and I—"

"Of course I knew her. I worked for Theresa," Michelle said. "I was Nate's nanny."

"Nate? He's John's son?"

Michelle nodded. "Stepson."

"Oh, I didn't..." I stopped and thought how foolish I felt for having to ask simple details I should've already had on my own. "Do they still live around here?"

Michelle gave me a funny look, like I was asking a dumb question. "*They?*"

"Nate? And his mom?"

The permanent smile she seemed to keep on her face disappeared. "Theresa passed away a few years ago."

Again, I felt it was information I should have already gathered before showing up to question John Thompson's widow. But admittedly, I was learning on the job. Not that I wanted it to appear as obvious as it had. "I'll call you. Good luck at your match." I held up the container of cookies. "And thanks for these."

Chapter 5

I WALKED UP TO the bar at a place called River's Edge Bistro, which turned out to be a misnomer since it wasn't close enough to the river to be considered at the "river's edge." It was actually a few miles from the St. Johns River, and as far as I could tell, there wasn't even a small creek nearby.

The place was quiet, and the bartender asked me what I wanted as soon as I sat down. She said, "I'm Lydia."

"Henry," I said. I ordered a beer.

"I've never seen you in here before," she said, twisting the top of a beer and placing it in front of me.

I said, "I don't think I've ever been. Maybe once before, but it was a different place."

She reached down and opened the door of the bar's under-counter dishwasher. Steam rose up as she slid a tray of hot glasses out, wiping each down before stacking them on the bar. She said, "Are you from Jax?"

"Fernandina Beach. I live at the Trout River Marina."

She nodded, and I could tell by her expression, she may not have been listening to what I said. "Be right back," she said, and walked away. She walked down the other end of the bar and poured two drinks for a couple across from her.

On her way back, I waved her over. "Can I ask you a question?"

Lydia went to the register, stuck a couple of bills inside the drawer, and came over. "Sure?"

"Do you know a man named John Thompson? I heard he used to come in here?"

The smile on her face disappeared. "Of course I do." Lydia looked toward the other end, where the couple was seated with their drinks. "See that seat over there, third from the end? That was John's seat."

"I'd heard he came in here," I said. "But I didn't know he was a regular?"

"I wouldn't call him a regular. That kind of has a negative connotation, doesn't it? John wasn't like that."

I shook my head. "No, I didn't mean it like that. I—"

"John had friends here, that's all. He'd stop for a drink after work, or later, if he had late meetings. Sometimes he'd have one drink and go home. Sometimes he'd stay for a while."

"Did he always come alone?"

"Sometimes," she said. "But, like I said, he had friends here."

"And as far as you know, he got along with everyone?"

Lydia nodded. "Mostly. Yes." She leaned on the counter, toward me, looking into my eyes. "You have nice eyes."

I couldn't tell if the compliment that came out of left field was an attempt to throw me off my questioning, or if she was being friendly. I lifted my glass to my mouth. "Thanks."

A man came in and sat a few stools down from me. Lydia went right to the tap and poured a beer, placing it down in front of him. "Hi, Joe," she said. She walked back over to me. "So, you mind if I ask *you* something?" She stood straight, arms crossed. "What's with all the questions about John Thompson?"

I pulled one of my business cards from my pocket and slid it across the bar.

Lydia picked it up. "So you're a private investigator, huh?" She looked at the door to the kitchen, then leaned with her hands out wide on the bar. "So, what are you investigating? The accident?"

I lifted the bottle to my lips, watching her. "You could say that."

"But what's there to investigate? He got hurt on his bike, right?" She reached for a cocktail napkin and dabbed the corner of her eye as a tear came down her cheek.

"I'm sorry," I said. "I didn't mean to upset you."

She wiped her nose with the napkin. "He was a good person. We all liked him. It's just... it's hard to believe." A man yelled for Lydia from somewhere in the kitchen. "I'll be right back." She walked away and through the door.

She returned two minutes later, carrying a case of beer she set on top of the cooler behind the bar. She said, "So who are you working for? The sheriff's office?"

"No, not the sheriff's office," I said. "But I need to keep my client's name confidential for now." I picked up my beer and finished what was left.

"Oh," is all she said, opening the top of the box, removing the bottles and putting them away on one side of the cooler. "So, why would you be investigating anything if it was a freak accident?"

I hadn't expected to be the one answering questions when I first walked in, but Lydia seemed to be very interested.

"I'm trying to pull together the details," I said.

But she wasn't going to stop asking her questions. "Is it because you think something else might've happened?" None of the other patrons seemed to be paying her much attention at that point. With her voice hushed, she said, "Do you think he was murdered?"

But even with her voice low, the other customers at the bar clearly heard her, all looking up from their drinks.

I grinned as their eyes all came toward me.

I leaned closer to Lydia. "All I'm trying to do is get to know a little more about John, understand a little about the people in his life. For now, I'm not ready to say it was anything other than what the sheriff's office has concluded."

"You mean, that it was an accident?"

I noticed a man looking at me through the small, round window on the door. I could only see his bald head from where I was, on top of his thick tree-trunk-like neck.

He stared at me but disappeared from the window for a moment, until the door swung open, and he stuck his head through. "Lydia," he said. "Come back here."

Lydia followed him and disappeared from my view.

I watched the TV on the wall and thought about having one more beer. Sometimes it was hard to sit in a bar and only have one, although I started to think about maybe having something a little stronger.

Lydia came back through the kitchen door.

"Everything all right?" I said. "He looked like he was staring at me; I thought maybe whatever he wanted might've had something to do with me."

She said, "He asked me who you were. And—what you wanted."

I grabbed my tab from across the bar and stuck a twenty under my glass. "I thought this was a bar," I said. "Did you tell him I came for a drink?"

She stared back at me. No answer.

I said, "Is he the boss?"

She nodded.

I stood from the stool and took out a ten, slipped it under my empty bottle. "Well, tell your boss he wants to ask questions about me next time I'm in here, tell him he can do it himself." I pointed at my business card she'd left on the bar. "If there's

33

anything else you want to share with me about John—anything at all—give me a call."

I stepped outside into the bright sun, the heat from it beating down on the sidewalk, with the humidity thicker than it was when I'd walked in.

I turned the corner around the building, heading toward my car in the parking lot out back but stopped when I realized I'd left my keys. I was going to go back inside, but the man—the boss from the kitchen—started toward me.

He dangled my keys, then folded his muscle-packed arms in front of his chest. "Looking for something?"

I walked toward him with my hand out. "Thanks for bringing them out," I said. But I knew he wanted something else by the way he held my keys in his closed fist.

The man was younger than me, dressed in a white T-shirt, tight to his body. He looked like Mr. Clean but not nearly as tall. This guy was shorter than me by at least a head, but his muscle-bound body made up for it.

"Why are you asking about John Thompson?"

"I didn't think there'd be any problem," I said. "Unless you have something to hide?"

He tilted his head, a smirk on his face. He took a step toward me. "You have something you're trying to say, buddy?"

"You couldn't hear me? I said I didn't think it'd be a problem, but maybe you have something to hide?"

I hadn't expected what came next. The man took one long step toward me, throwing a punch so hard, it felt like I'd been kicked by a mule. My head whipped back, and I stumbled, reaching for my jaw as I straightened out.

He came at me with another swing, but I'd turned my chin this time, taking a shot to the side of my head. My ears were ringing as the man grabbed me by the shirt. He threw me down to the ground, then dropped his knee into my stomach.

I looked up at the blinding sun glowing around his big head.

He dropped my keys on my chest and got off me. He turned and started to walk away.

But I jumped up and onto my feet, reached for his head and spun him around. I drove my forehead square into his face with a loud pop.

Blood immediately started to drip from his nose. He covered his face with both hands, the blood streaming through his fingers. "You broke my nose! You broke my goddamn nose."

He raised his fist, about to throw another punch, but I came up with a hook and caught him under the chin, then swung my leg and took him out by his feet.

He hit the asphalt hard, and with my keys in my hand, I ran for my car. I jumped in, turned the ignition, and spun the car around, tires squealing as I took off from the parking lot. I glanced in the rearview and saw my new friend stumbling, his face bloodied, trying to get to his feet.

· · · ● · ● · ● · ·

Alex was out on her front porch when I arrived at her house, after calling her. Her dog, Raz, a full-sized Shepherd-Retriever mix she adopted after fostering him for a few months, barked and charged down the stairs when he saw me, but stopped dead in his tracks, tail wagging. His aggressive pace became a happy trot.

"C'mere, Raz," I said. I crouched down to pet him.

Alex stood up from the rocking chair and walked down the steps toward me. "Are you okay?"

"I left my keys on the bar at River's Edge. The owner was nice enough to bring them out to me, but I guess he felt a good fight was a fair trade-off."

Alex stared back at me, her eyes wide. She grabbed me by the arm and pulled me through the doorway and inside the house. We went into the kitchen and she sat me on a stool at the pub-style table under the window.

She grabbed a towel from a drawer, grabbed some ice she wrapped in the towel, and handed it to me as she looked closer at my head. "That's a good lump," she said. "You sure you didn't do anything to instigate this?"

"All I did was go in, ask the bartender about John Thompson. This dude was in the kitchen watching me."

"Maybe he's her boyfriend? Could be he doesn't like good-looking men talking to his woman." Alex grinned.

I shook my head. "All she said was he's the boss. Besides, she's half my age." I held the ice up on the side of my head. "He didn't like me asking questions about John."

Alex's eyes opened wide. "Is that what he said?"

"That's *all* he said."

Alex left the kitchen and came right back with her laptop in her hand. She put it up on the table. "I looked him up when you called." She turned the screen toward me so I could see it. "Is this him?"

There was a photo of the same guy, posing as if he was in a bodybuilding competition.

"Yeah, that's him. Big dude, isn't he?"

She nodded. "You know his name?"

"No. We didn't have much of a chance to chat."

"Well, I do. His last name's Mason. Brian Mason. He's Roy Mason's son."

I studied the photo and could almost see the resemblance, although Brian didn't appear to get his father's height.

Alex pulled a bottle of sparkling water from the refrigerator, poured a glass, and put it down in front of me.

I pulled the ice from my head. "Don't you have something stronger?"

She didn't answer. "So, that's a little strange, isn't it?" she said. "He attacks a paying customer for asking questions about John Thompson?"

I sipped the water and looked out the window. "Seems a little suspicious, don't you think? This bartender, Lydia, seemed to be pretty upset about John. She made it sound like he was just one of her friendly customers, but I couldn't help but wonder if there was more to it."

Alex said, "Take a look at this."

I walked to the table and Alex showed me a picture of Roy Mason and John Thompson together. They held a large trophy between them.

"It's a golf tournament from last year," she said. "The article mentions that Roy is John's client and that they both sponsored the tournament. It mentions that Roy owns a lot of property and a few businesses throughout the Southeast."

"Angela said he's got his hands in a lot of businesses," I said. "Sounds like mostly real estate?"

"Mostly. He's involved in both commercial and private real estate development, but he has other businesses." She turned the laptop back and typed on the keyboard. "Do you know anything about John's second wife?"

I said, "She's dead. That's all I know."

Alex said, "She died in her home. She'd gotten back from a business trip, and John found her dead at the bottom of the stairs."

She turned the laptop toward me again, and I glanced over the article she'd found.

Alex said, "A year later, he married Michelle."

Chapter 6

ANGELA THOMPSON OPENED HER door, dressed much more casually than she was at her office, wearing shorts and a baggy, buttoned-down shirt that appeared too big for her, like it might've been a man's. She stood in bare feet, holding a glass of wine. "Thanks for coming out," she said, smiling as she backed from the door, holding it open. "Please, come inside."

I followed her inside and into her living room, left of the foyer. A baby grand piano caught my eye. I nodded toward it. "Do you play?"

"Not as much as I used to," she said.

The room had an oversized, brown leather couch loaded with a mismatch of pillows and two smaller love seats, surrounding a square, cushioned piece of furniture I wasn't sure was an ottoman or coffee table. The room had two levels, and in the lower section, one step down, was a small bar built into the wall, with four stools. The shelves behind the bar were stocked top to bottom with liquor.

Compared to John and Michelle's house, Angela's was more normal, modest sized. With a good portion of the walls covered in art, or shelves filled with books, there was something I liked about the place.

"How long have you lived here?" I said.

"John and I bought this house together. It was our first big purchase." She smiled, looking around the room. "I haven't changed things much, but it seems like it was yesterday. I remember it felt like we broke the bank at the time, when we could barely afford it. If I'd only known then what a house around here would be worth today, I would have bought more."

"It's nice," I said, looking over at the piano again.

She said, "Do you play?"

"I played when I was young. Can't fit a piano on my boat, so even if I wanted to..."

Angela laughed, and stepped down to the bar, walking around to the other side of it. "Can I get you a drink?" She topped off her glass of wine, then reached for a rocks glass from a shelf.

I hadn't answered her and didn't think I needed a drink at that point.

But with her back to me, she grabbed ice from the fridge and poured Jack Daniels.

She turned and slid it across the bar to me, smiling. "Two ice cubes."

Angela had a nice smile. I believed she was short of sixty, but she didn't look it.

I raised my drink to her and took a sip as Angela came back around to my side. She stepped up to the area with the couch and sat down, patting the cushion next to her. "Please, come have a seat." She watched me step up and come toward her, but I sat in the love seat to her left.

She had a sly smile on her face, sipping her wine. "I'd like to apologize again for yesterday? I try not to ever let something like that happen, but I—"

"No, really. It's fine," I said. "I'm here now."

Angela moved over, so she was closer to me on the other couch. "There's a lot of hand-holding involved with someone like Roy. He demands the attention, considering what he pays us. But before John died, he was the one who handled Roy's account. Now it all falls in my lap. I'm the one who'll have to deal with him for eternity."

"Speaking of Roy," I said. "I met his son."

"Brian?"

"I wasn't aware he had more than one," I said.

"He, well... Roy had another son, but he was killed in an ATV accident when he was four years old."

"Four years old? What was he doing riding an ATV?"

Angela closed her eyes for a brief moment, shaking her head. "It was such a tragedy. You'd think something like that would destroy a man, but Roy never let anyone see that side of him, if it had. He doesn't like to show a soft side, if he even has one." She sipped her wine. "He's what you'd call a man's man."

"Was John like that, too?" I said.

Angela laughed and tucked her bare foot under her other leg, turning to face me. "John wasn't even close to being what you'd call a man's man. But you could call him a *ladies'* man. Which is what got him into trouble for most of his life."

I understood what she was saying and thought about the admiration, Lydia, the bartender, seemed to show for John. I said, "Were John and Roy alike in any ways? It doesn't sound like it."

"Not at all, really. Roy likes his Budweiser and only buys something if it's made in America. John liked Paris, fine wine, and foreign cars."

"But they still got along well?"

Angela paused before she answered. "I'd say so."

I said, "Roy made it sound like they were the closest of friends. But did that have more to do with them being business associates? I know plenty of people in business who treat their clients like family until the business relationship comes to an end. Then it's as if they never even knew each other."

"I don't know," Angela said. "I know what you're saying. It's all a part of being in the business world. Sometimes you have to fake it a little. So, I guess I'd say maybe it was a little of both." She got up from the couch and stepped back down to the bar. Her glass of wine wasn't empty, but she topped it off anyway.

She went around the other side and grabbed the bottle of Jack. "Would you like another?"

I finished what was left in my glass and walked over to the bar. "I'm all right for now," I said, trying hard to be disciplined. I always felt having a full bar in your home was dangerous. "I did go see Michelle, by the way. And she mentioned that the two of you don't get along very well."

Angela huffed out a laugh and rolled her eyes. "That's just Michelle being Michelle. She's always been a little paranoid. I think she's afraid of me."

I said, "She told me you and she rarely talked."

"What exactly would you have liked us to talk about?"

I thought for a moment. "I don't know. I guess the fact you and John were business partners, and he was still a part of your life. The fact she'd never even been to your office..."

"She told you that?"

"Is it not true?" I said.

Angela brushed her hair from her face before taking a drink from her glass. "Maybe not. I guess I never paid enough attention to whether or not she'd been in the office. I'm not sure why it even matters, to be honest." She finished her wine and poured what little was left in the bottle into her glass. She walked around to my side and leaned with one elbow on the bar, facing me. "You were starting to tell me about how you met Brian," she said. "But I should be honest with you; I already knew about it. Roy called me, told me what happened. He said you broke Brian's nose."

She didn't look upset or disappointed, but held her gaze, like she wanted to hear my side of the story.

"He followed me out the door and came looking for a fight. He said he didn't like the idea I was there asking questions about John."

She sighed. "Brian's always been a little hot under the collar. Even when he was a kid. But you have to understand where he's coming from."

"Which is where? I guess I'm not sure," I said.

"John meant something to Brian. You know how some kids will call friends of their parents their aunt or uncle? To Brian, John was Uncle John."

"So it wasn't just business," I said. "Can you tell me who else you think I should be talking to? His best friend, his widow... I need something more. And I can't help but think there's something you're not telling me."

Angela stared back at me without a word, then straightened up from the bar and moved back to the couch.

"What is it?" I said. "Please, I can't do this if you're not going to be up front with me. I need to know, whatever you can tell me. I know he was well-liked. But he must've had some enemies."

"Of course," she said. "When you stay in the same business and live in the same place for most of your adult life, it's impossible not to step on someone's toes."

"But there's nobody that stands out? You don't have a single person you can think of?"

She said, "All I can tell you is when I heard John had died out there at the park, the first thought that entered my mind was somebody must've killed him."

Chapter 7

I HADN'T SLEPT MUCH throughout the night and got out of bed at the same time the sun had cracked the horizon. It was quiet in the marina, other than the fishing boats heading out. I thought about calling Alex to see if she was awake but decided I'd rather send a text:

Call me when you get up.

I knew she'd gone out with Mike Stone the night before, while I was at Angela's, and couldn't help but wonder what, if anything, was really going on between them. Alex assured me there was nothing between them, considering the fact Mike was closer to her father's age. But age didn't always matter, so I always had it in the back of my mind that there was a chance, whatever their relationship was, at the time, could turn into something more meaningful.

Not that I was jealous or anything.

I went out onto the dock with a lawn chair and my coffee, placing the chair facing east, where the sun had risen over the river. The orange glow coming from the clouds reflected off the water.

Living on a boat wasn't for everyone, but it was hard to beat the morning view.

I thought about John and Michelle Thompson and kept wondering about the bartender, Lydia. I could help but think there was something there. Lydia made it clear John wasn't just some everyday regular hanging out at a bar. Maybe there wasn't much more to it, and I was overthinking. I wondered about John's brother and how Angela stated the fact that Eric and John barely got along, even though John had given him a job. Roy and his son kept me thinking.

My phone buzzed in my pocket.

I had a text from Alex:

I'm up.

A second later, the phone rang, and it was Alex. I answered, and said, "I didn't wake you, did I?"

She took a moment or two to answer, yawning into the phone. "Actually, yes, you did."

I sipped my coffee and watched a boat going past, on the river. "You're missing a beautiful morning on the St. Johns."

"I'm missing a beautiful morning of sleep," she said. "It's too early."

I laughed.

She said, "You say you wake up early because you like that everyone else is asleep."

Fishing boats were leaving the marina. "Besides the fishermen."

"Right," she said. "But then why do you always call me if you like to be up, alone?"

I had to think about it. "You want me to let you go back to sleep? You can call me later if—"

"I'm up now," she said.

"Can you meet? There was something Angela said last night when I was over there, has me thinking."

"I was wondering how it went," Alex said. "What'd she say?"

I sipped my coffee, then tossed the rest over the edge of the dock, into the river. "Come over when you can," I said.

Alex was quiet, the phone sounding muffled, like she'd rolled over in the sheets. She said, "I gotta walk Raz, take a shower... Can you give me an hour? And how about we meet at the Coffee Ground?"

She knew I didn't always have the tea she liked. And my coffee was never very good.

I said, "See you in an hour."

• • • • ● • ● • • •

I sat at a table under an umbrella on the patio outside the Coffee Ground, a trendy coffee joint right on West Bay. Halfway through my first cup of coffee, Alex finally showed up in flip-flops, shorts, and a tank top.

"Morning," I said.

48

Alex seemed to struggle with a smile, pulling out the chair across from me. She plopped down into her seat.

"Are you all right?" I said.

"I'm tired."

"Okay, well, you're up now," I said, standing from the chair. "Let me get you a tea."

She waved me off and stood, starting toward the glass-doored entrance. "I'll get it. Be right back."

I sat back into my chair and sipped my coffee, looking toward the street. It was barely past seven, and the commuters were already out on the road. The only way to beat the heavy traffic in Jacksonville was to get up and out early. And the only way to beat the people trying to beat the traffic was to get up before the sun had risen.

Alex was back out a few minutes later with her tea.

"What'd you get?" I said.

Alex raised her paper cup. "Mint green with some kind of black tea, for the caffeine." She smiled and peeled the top off, steam rising up from the surface.

I said, "I don't know how you drink green tea by itself anyway. It's like sipping water from a leaf-clogged gutter."

She rolled her eyes and laughed, removing her sunglasses. As tired as she was, Alex's brown eyes had the same glow they always had.

"So, tell me about Angela," she said.

"She drinks a lot," I said. "More than me."

Alex looked like she wasn't buying it. She kept quiet, especially since my drinking was often a touchy subject. It wasn't that I had a drinking problem. At least I didn't think so. But Alex, as much as she liked a drink herself, would often make comments like my mother would if she saw me having one too many.

"She has a nice house," I said. "It's the house she bought with John when they were first married. It's not even half the size of the one Michelle and John lived in. And it has more character than those big cookie-cutter McMansions."

Alex said, "The man was on his third wife. A big house sounds like it might've fit his personality." She sipped her tea.

"Roy had already called her, upset about what happened with me and his son. It sounds like he has a broken nose."

"Oh, that's not good," Alex said. "Especially with Roy Mason already being hostile, from what you said, to Angela hiring you."

I pushed my coffee aside and leaned on the table. "Something else she said caught my ear, right before I left. She said when she first found out John had died, her first thought was that someone must've killed him."

Alex's eyes went wide. "Did she elaborate?"

"Not really. No names, if that's what you mean."

"That's all she said? Without any details?"

"I think she was trying to make it clear John may have had some enemies. Maybe quite a few," I said.

Alex leaned back in the chair.

"Roy and John were friends, of course. But she said the two were total opposites. But the bar where John liked to hang out, even though Angela said he liked his fine wines and perhaps fancier establishments... that bar is somewhat more of a dive bar. I mean, it's nothing fancy. You'd think a guy like John, with all his money, wouldn't hang out at such a place."

Alex said, "But his friend's son owns the place. That's a good enough reason for him to hang out there, isn't it?"

I picked up my coffee and gazed out toward the street. "I keep thinking about the young woman behind the bar, Lydia." I paused, not sure it made sense to even say what I'd wanted to.

"Thinking *what*?" Alex said. "That there might've been something going on between them?"

I grabbed my cup, thinking. "It's possible."

"And you said she's a lot younger than John?"

"Much younger," I said. "Early twenties. But he seemed to like them like that."

"Young?"

I nodded.

Alex said, "I imagine she's attractive?"

"She's a cute kid, sure. And probably a bit flirtatious."

Alex laughed. "Did she hit on you? Maybe if she likes older men..."

"No, she didn't. She was, uh, complimentary."

"Toward you?" She rolled her eyes but didn't say much else.

A car with a loud muffler went by on the street, the smell from it just about choking me.

51

I said, "Do you want to come over to John's brother's house? I want to catch him before he goes to work. Angela said he doesn't get in until after nine or ten. So if he's up, now would be a good time to swing by."

Alex nodded. "I'll drive."

I said, "Good, because I walked here."

"You walked? From the marina?"

The marina wasn't far, but it wasn't close, either. It was a thirty-minute walk. "I needed to clear my head," I said.

We left the patio, walking side by side on the sidewalk, without saying much until we got to her Jeep.

I said, "So how was your date with Detective Stone?"

She stepped up into her Jeep, staring at me as I jumped up into the passenger side. She said, "How many times do I have to tell you; it's never a date when I go out with Mike. We're just friends. And even if there *was* more to it..." She let out a sigh, turning her key in the ignition. "He did come right out and ask me if you were somehow involved with John Thompson's case. He'd heard about it from someone; I don't know who."

I said, "So what'd you say?"

She pulled out from the parking space and onto the street. "I wasn't going to lie to him."

"Why not?" I said, half kidding.

"Don't worry," she said. "I told him you were doing some insurance work for Angela."

"Does he know you're helping me?"

We stopped at a red light, and she shifted toward me. "He asked, but I said I wasn't. But the look he gave me... I'm pretty sure he knew I was lying."

Chapter 8

IT WAS FIVE PAST eight in the morning when Alex and I pulled into the driveway at Eric Thompson's townhouse. There were no cars in the driveway, which meant he either used his garage, or nobody was home. Angela had described Eric as a grown man who lived like a frat boy.

I stretched to look up through the small window in the garage door and saw a black Acura NSX parked inside.

I walked up the steps ahead of Alex to the front door and rang the doorbell. I didn't hear any sounds from inside.

After a minute, waiting, I rang the bell again. This time the door opened.

Eric stood behind the glass storm door, dressed in gym shorts and a faded, red Coca-Cola T-shirt. His hair stuck up in all directions, and one eye was practically closed. He yawned, then pushed open the door and stuck his head outside. "Yes?"

"Eric, I don't know if you remember us, but..."

"You're that PI, right? The one Angela hired." His eyes moved to Alex. "And you brought your hot sidekick. Just like on TV." He laughed.

I was sure Alex didn't like the idea of being called a "sidekick," but she gave me a look, like I could let it slide.

Eric said, "So what do you want?" He rubbed his eyes with both hands like a little boy would, then squinted from the sun as it came up over the house across the street. "What time is it?"

I said, "It's ten past eight. We wanted to catch you before you left for work."

"Catch me?" He laughed. "Catch me doing *what*... Magnum?"

I guessed he was trying to be funny, but I wasn't sure I liked the joke. I put my foot up on the first step. "Do you mind if we ask you some questions?"

He gave himself a once-over. "I'm still in my pajamas. But if this is about my brother, I'm not sure I have much to talk about. I'm not even sure what you're trying to accomplish, other than getting some cash out of Angela. Or maybe keep her happy, so she'll have someone to blame."

"How about we wait right here and give you a few minutes to get cleaned up—if you want to—and then if you give us a few minutes of your morning, we'll be out of your hair."

Eric didn't respond. He was staring at Alex in a very creepy way. "So, is your real name *Alex*? Or is it Alex*andria*?"

"You can call me Alex," she said.

"But isn't it short for something? It must be Alexandria, no?"

Alex stared up at him but wasn't going to give him the satisfaction of getting into it.

"I like girls with boys' names," Eric said. "It's cute."

I saw Alex adjust the holster she'd worn under her shirt, and worried she'd pull her Glock, shoot the man right in the chest.

I looked Eric in the eye. "Why don't you show a little respect?"

He said, "You show up at my door, wake me out of bed, and you expect me to lay out the red carpet? You want me to fix you some breakfast, too?"

I kept my gaze on him, feeling a rush through my body like I wasn't going to be able to help smacking the guy. "Listen, all we're asking is for you to answer a few questions about your brother." I looked past him into his house. "Unless you're hiding something?"

Last person I said that to, punched me in the face. But Eric didn't appear to be the type. More like a punk who liked to do a lot of talking but nothing more.

Eric shook his head. "I don't have anything to hide," he said. "And I don't appreciate whatever it is you're implying."

I said, "It's just that, when someone's afraid to answer a few simple questions after the death of someone close, they're either in deep mourning, or want to keep a secret." I gave him a nod. "I hate to say it, but you don't seem to be in deep mourning."

He swallowed, nodding his head. "Wait here, let me get cleaned up." He started to close the door, but stopped. "What's your name again? Harry?"

I said, "You can call me whatever you'd like."

* * *

Fifteen minutes had gone by since Eric had gone in to get cleaned up. Alex was back in the driver's seat of her Jeep, her head back with her sunglasses over her eyes. I was afraid she'd fallen asleep.

I paced back and forth in front of Eric's door. "You think he went back to bed?"

Alex lifted her head, clearly awake. But before she answered, the door opened.

Eric had on the same shorts with the Coca-Cola T-shirt. He hadn't even changed. "I only have a few minutes." He turned and let the door slam behind him.

Alex got out of the Jeep, and we walked in after Eric.

The place smelled like stale beer and microwaved burritos. Maybe it wasn't burritos, but that's what I pictured when I walked down the hall, toward the kitchen. A plastic garbage barrel pushed against the wall was filled with empty beer cans.

Eric had his back to us, pouring himself a coffee at the kitchen counter. He turned back around as he took a sip from his cup. "Go ahead, ask away."

I expected maybe there'd be a kitchen table or at least a stool for someone to sit on. I said, "Do you live here alone?"

He nodded. "I do now. I bought the place with an old girlfriend." He leaned against the counter with one bare foot crossed over the other, holding the cup at his chest. "Does that count as your first question? If I live here with anyone? Because, like I said, I don't have much time."

Eric straightened himself out, turned, and put his cup behind him on the counter.

I said, "I didn't know your brother personally, but it looks to me you had two different lifestyles. So why don't you first tell me what kind of relationship you had with your brother? Maybe, start with simply telling us how well you and your brother got along?"

"*How well we got along?*" He shrugged. "Are you hoping I'll say we hated each other? So you could start to think maybe I killed him?" He huffed out a laugh and picked up his coffee.

I said, "If you could answer at least one question without a smart-ass remark, we'll get this over with a lot sooner."

He looked out the window toward the back of the townhouse. He said, "I'm afraid you're wasting your time. My brother's death was an accident. There's really no need for you to—"

"That's for me to decide," I said. "But what if Angela's right? What if we find something about your brother that proves his death was something more?"

"But you have no proof of anything," he said. "You don't even have a suspect, do you? The only reason you're here, so you know, is because Angela's paranoid. She's so paranoid, she had to go out and hire some washed-up ex-cop?"

The thought crossed my mind to grab him by the shirt and throw him to the floor. But I knew that wouldn't get me very far, and make it less likely the man would cooperate in any way.

But I kept calm. "Is there anyone out there who might've had a problem with John?"

"A problem?" Eric shrugged. "John was no saint. But I can't think of anybody who'd want to kill him. It doesn't make any sense, so—"

"You can't think of anything or anyone, through his business? Or in his personal life, where he might've had some kind of issue?"

"The biggest issue he had was with his partner."

I said, "You mean, Michelle?"

Eric shook his head. "No, not his *wife*. His *partner*. His *business* partner. The *other* Mrs. Thompson."

"Angela?"

He nodded. "Those two'd been at each other's throats for, well, for as long as they'd been together. The way they'd acted, sometimes was as if they were still together. They fought like an old married couple, as if they'd stayed married all those years."

Chapter 9

BILLY WAS SEATED DOWN at the far end of his bar by himself, away from customers, his head down in a laptop. He removed a pair of glasses from his face.

Alex and I sat down at the opposite end.

"What are you doing down there?" I said.

"Paying bills," he said. "My favorite part of the week."

Alex said to Billy, "When did you start wearing glasses?"

He shrugged, looking over the glasses in his hand. "I didn't think I was already at the age where I needed glasses to be able to see what's right in front of me."

Alex smiled. "Put them on. Let me see."

Billy put the glasses on. "I wouldn't mind wearing them if I didn't think they made me look like an old man."

"Not bad," Alex said.

I laughed. "Yeah, not bad for an old man."

"You wait," Billy said. "Your time will come. One day you'll come in here, you won't be able to see the menu. I'll be there to call *you* an old man."

We both laughed.

The door to the bathroom opened behind Billy. One of the regulars, Old Man Earl, walked out with a newspaper under his arm.

Alex waved toward the other side of the bar. "How are you doing, Earl?"

He sat a couple of stools down from Billy and smiled back at Alex.

"I'm not bad, beautiful."

Earl was at this same bar at a much younger age when Billy's uncle owned the place, long before Billy took it over. It was a dumpy restaurant back then, before Billy had turned it into one of the more popular bars on the river.

Billy stood from the stool. "I'll be right back." He walked through the doorway and went up the stairs to his office.

Earl looked down the bar toward me and Alex. "So how are you two lovebirds doing?"

We both laughed.

"I don't know how many times I have to tell you, Earl. It's not like that."

Earl said, "Well then, you're crazy, Henry. If I were any younger..."

Billy came down the stairs and stepped behind the bar, tying an apron around his waist. "Lunch rush should be starting any minute."

Alex said, "You're all alone today?"

He said, "For now. Chloe called, said she'd be a little late. Hopefully she's here before it gets too busy for me."

The front doors opened, and in walked a group of at least a dozen men and women, mostly gray or white haired. They weren't all together, but Billy's was a popular place for the snowbirds from the Northeast, and they normally showed up for lunch well before noon. Usually right around eleven thirty.

"Like clockwork," Billy said. He walked toward me and leaned with his hands on the bar. "Someone was in here looking for you last night."

"Oh yeah? You get a name?"

Billy shook his head. "He was a young kid. Early twenties, maybe. He didn't say his name, and I didn't ask. He wanted to know if I knew where to find you, but I told him I'd give you a message. He left without saying anything else."

I wondered who the kid could've been.

I said, "What'd he look like?"

Billy grabbed a stack of menus from under the bar and held them in his hands, looking toward the crowd waiting by the door for tables. "He had light-brown hair. Almost blond. Medium build, maybe five ten or eleven, if I had to guess."

"Did he stick around, have a drink or anything?"

"He didn't," Billy said. "Too bad. I would've checked his ID and gotten you his name."

Billy started to walk from behind the bar. "You sticking around?"

"We're heading out to Losco Park."

"Where John Thompson was killed?"

I nodded. "We'll be back for lunch, in a couple of hours."

• • • ● • ● ● • •

We were on Route 95, a little past Southside, when I looked in my rearview at a white pickup I was starting to think had been following us since we'd left the parking lot at Billy's Place.

I knew Alex was watching me.

"What's wrong?" she said.

I kept my eyes in the rearview. "I think we're being followed."

Alex looked toward the side-view mirror. "Which car?"

"The white pickup. It looks like an F-150, maybe a 250." I said. "And I don't like that bull bar on the front."

She slouched down in the passenger seat, looking toward the side-view mirror. "Are you sure?"

I said, "That they're following us?" I gave her a quick look but didn't respond. I *wasn't* sure.

"Windshield's dark," I said. "I can't even make out a face."

I pushed the pedal down and picked up speed, trying to create some distance between my Toyota and the pickup following close behind.

Alex said, "Maybe we should turn off somewhere, see if they follow?" She pulled her Glock from the holster.

I agreed it was a good idea, and we drove straight past the exit for Losco Park, heading east on 295. I turned off onto the Greenland Road exit, going west. Looking in the mirror, I saw the truck had followed.

"Whoever it is... is still behind us."

After a couple of miles, I turned again, this time down Fayal Drive. It took us into an industrial park.

Alex said, "Do you know where you're going?"

"Not at all." I didn't see the truck in the rearview. "But I think we lost our tail."

Alex kneeled on her seat and turned, her Glock in her hand, looking behind us and all around. "Are we being paranoid?" She laughed, settling back in her seat.

"But where'd the truck go?" I said. "It was behind us off the exit."

Maybe she was right and we were being paranoid.

I took a sharp turn down an old road that had more grass than asphalt. Most of the lots we passed were enclosed with broken chain-link fences and overgrown with weeds and half-dead trees. I stopped at a crossroad without a single stop sign; the road ahead had a sharp turn that disappeared somewhere beyond the trees. An old, wooden sign with a faded-red arrow pointing to the right said Harbor Industries.

I put the car in park and turned off the engine. "Let's wait a few minutes, see if anyone shows up."

Alex again turned in her seat and looked toward the rear of the car. I grabbed my phone to check the GPS and make sure I knew where we were. I heard the loud roar of an engine, tires squealing. The white pickup truck appeared out of nowhere and was driving straight at us, dirt and dust flying up all around it.

I turned the engine over, but my car wouldn't start. I yelled, "Get out!" and I pushed Alex toward the passenger door. "Hurry!" She saw the truck and reached for the passenger door as I turned and pushed open the driver's-side door.

I jumped from the car and ran, diving out of the way as the truck made impact, smashing the front end of the Camry with an explosive sound, packed with such force, it likely pushed the engine straight through to the front seat. The Toyota flipped end over end and spun backward, then stopped, landing on its side and up against a chain-link fence.

I watched it all while on my back, with blood on my hands and drips coming down from somewhere on my head. There was sharp pain in the back of my skull.

I jumped to my feet and watched the white truck disappear around the corner.

My Toyota was destroyed. But that was the least of my concerns. I ran across the road, screaming for Alex.

She didn't answer.

"Alex!" I yelled, my vision a hectic blur. I couldn't focus. "Where are you?" I looked toward the overgrown grass along the fence. "Alex!" I didn't see her anywhere.

Please tell me you got out.

I ran toward the Camry. Smoke poured out from inside. "Alex!" Black smoke poured through the smashed windshield. I couldn't see her, and the smell of gasoline grew stronger. "Alex! Can you hear me?"

The ground was littered with metal and plastic and glass—pieces of my Toyota.

I ran back to where we were stopped when the truck crashed into the car. I couldn't catch my breath. "Alex?"

I heard my name.

It was Alex, her voice almost in a whisper. "Henry... help."

I ran toward her voice and saw her feet coming out from behind a fallen tree. I dropped down and kneeled next to her. "Can you hear me?"

Her eyes were closed, but she opened them and reached for my shoulder. She tried to sit up, and I put my arm behind her to help.

"Are you okay?"

She nodded, blood coming down her face.

"Where does it hurt?"

She shrugged and touched her face, looking at the blood on the tips of her fingers. "Everywhere."

66

Chapter 10

ALEX AND I WALKED along Greenland Road as Jacksonville Fire and Rescue vehicles sped past us, sirens screaming. The sheriff's vehicles were right behind. I turned to see smoke rising into the air.

Alex held my T-shirt against the back of her head.

I said, "We should've waited for the EMTs, have them look you over."

"I'm fine," she said, looking up ahead at the Lexus driving toward us.

Billy was behind the wheel.

He pulled over to the side of the road and jumped out from his car, looking somewhat panicked as he hurried over to Alex. "Are you all right?" He looked at the bloodied towel and faced me. "She needs a doctor." He opened the back passenger door. "Get in."

He grabbed a clean towel and a clear plastic bag filled with ice and handed them to Alex, then tossed me a T-shirt that had Billy's Place printed on the front. "Cover yourself up, will you?"

I pulled the T-shirt on and got in back with Alex. I didn't want her to sit back there alone. "Let's go to the hospital," I said. "Make sure you're all right." I took the bloodied T-shirt from her.

Alex said, "I'm telling you, I'm fine. All I want to do is find that truck, find that son of a—"

"We'll find him, Alex. But not right now," said Billy as he stepped in behind the wheel and turned his Lexus around.

Alex closed her eyes.

"Hey," I said, my hand on her leg. "Keep your eyes open, okay?"

She nodded but didn't open her eyes. The bleeding seemed to have stopped, but I was worried.

I took the ice from her hand and held it on her head. "Does this hurt?"

She took the ice and pushed my hand away. She mumbled, "Henry, stop. I'm okay." She opened her eyes.

Billy said, "You should call the sheriff's office. I'm sure they're looking for you."

• • • ● • ● • • •

Billy pulled the Lexus into Baptist Medical Center and followed the signs toward the emergency room entrance.

My phone rang. "There he is," I said, turning to Alex. "It's Mike." I let it ring, unsure if I really wanted to answer it.

In a quiet voice, Alex told me to answer it.

"Walsh Investigations," I said, acting like I didn't know it was him.

"Walsh?" he said in his deep, raspy voice. "Mike Stone."

"Oh, hello, Detective. What a surprise."

"Cut the crap, Walsh. Where are you?"

"Where *am* I?" I paused. "Why?"

"Just got off the phone with one of our officers. There's a mess down in an industrial park south of 295, off Greenland Road. He ran a plate on a pile of burning metal they found tipped over back there. And wouldn't you know it, it just so happens to be your car."

"My car? You sure?"

"No games, Walsh. There was blood at the scene, but no sign of anyone. Clearly, you're not dead."

"Sorry," I said.

"You'd better start talking, Walsh."

Billy pulled up to the sliding doors outside the emergency center's entrance.

"Mike, I gotta go. I can't talk right now." I was about to hang up, but he yelled through the phone.

"Don't hang up on me, Walsh. You'd better tell me what the hell's going on!"

69

I held the phone up to my ear and stepped out to help Alex from the car. "I'm serious, Mike. I gotta go. I'm at the ER. I'm with Alex. She was in the car with me."

"What? What happened? What emergency room?"

Alex walked ahead of me with Billy helping her.

"I gotta go." I reached for Alex's arm.

Mike snapped. "Tell me what hospital!"

"Baptist Medical."

"Which one?"

"South."

I hung up and helped Alex to a chair in the waiting area, then hurried to the front desk.

· · · ● · ● · ● ● · ·

The doors at the entrance slid open, and Mike Stone, toothpick hanging from his mouth, walked right past me and Billy in the waiting area. I didn't know if he saw us or pretended he didn't. He headed straight for the woman behind the desk.

"I'm here about a patient," he said. "Her name's Alex Jepson."

The nurse tapped on the keyboard, then looked at Mike. "She's still with the doctor. If you want to have a seat, I'll let you know as soon as we have more information."

He started to pull his badge from his wallet but glanced over his shoulder, looking toward me and Billy. He pulled the toothpick from his mouth. "Walsh?" He walked toward us. "You'd better start talking."

I stood from the chair. "She's fine."

"Goddamnit, Walsh, tell me what happened before I—"

"She's getting stitched. Had a pretty good cut on the back of her head. They're running tests for a potential concussion. But they weren't sure when I spoke with the nurse."

I said to Billy, "You remember Detective Stone, don't you?"

They both exchanged a nod.

Mike said, "Billy, from Billy's Place?"

Billy nodded.

Mike said to me, "I saw your car. At least what's left of it. I'm guessing Alex wasn't inside, or we'd be looking at something much worse than a concussion. "Witness from one of the businesses back there said they saw two people walking away from the scene." He pulled another toothpick from his pocket, sticking it in his mouth. "Can you explain to me why you'd run from the scene if you weren't up to something you shouldn't have been."

"They were both in shock," Billy said.

Mike gave him a look like he wasn't asking him, pulled the toothpick from his mouth, and held his gaze on me. "If I have to take you downtown..."

"Downtown? What'd you do, watch some cop movies last night? Who *says* that?"

Mike took a step toward me. We were close to the same size, although I'd admit he could be somewhat intimidating when

71

he wanted to be. Being the one with the badge might've given him the upper hand.

The door to the treatment area swung open, and a nurse stood looking at the clipboard in her hand. She looked right at me. "Henry Walsh? You can come back to see her now."

I smirked at Mike and walked away from him.

But he reached for my arm and tried to shove me aside. He had his badge in his hand and flashed it for the nurse. "I'm Detective Mike Stone with the Jacksonville Sheriff's Office." He gave me a look out of the corner of his eye. "I'd like to speak with Ms. Jepson. *Privately.*"

"Don't listen to him," I said. "It's not official *police* business."

The nurse looked at us like we were both a couple of dopes. She turned and started through the door. "You can all follow me."

Mike stepped ahead of me and walked right behind her. I stopped to hold the door, looking at Billy watching us. "You coming?"

He got up and followed us into the treatment area. Some of the small, individual treatment areas were empty, but most were enclosed by curtains. The nurse pulled open one of them.

There was a young doctor in there, and the nurse said, "We've got a whole gang here for her."

He raised his eyebrows, then turned back to Alex and smiled.

Alex was smiling.

"I'm Henry Walsh," I said, reaching out to shake the doctor's hand.

Mike gave him a nod. "I'm Detective Mike Stone."

Alex lifted her head from the pillow. "I'm sorry about the crowd."

The doctor faced the rest of us. "I was telling Alex the results came back negative for a concussion. But we stitched her up pretty good. Fifteen stitches." He said to Alex, "We'll keep you on that IV for another thirty minutes, then you can get out of here. You should rest for at least the next twenty-four hours. Okay? Try to take it easy."

I gave the doctor a nod as he walked away from us, then stepped closer to the bed, resting my hand on Alex's shoulder. "Are you okay?"

She nodded with a small grin.

Mike said, "So, who's going to tell me what happened?"

I said, "Didn't you hear the doctor? She needs to take it easy for twenty-four hours. What part of that didn't you understand?"

He narrowed his eyes and stared back at me, clenching his teeth. "I told you, if I have to take you downtown to get answers, I will."

Alex winced as she lifted her head from the pillow. "Just tell him..."

I stared back at her for a moment, then shifted my gaze to Mike. "We were followed by someone driving a Ford. Pretty sure it was an F-250. Unless he was simply a bad driver, I'm pretty sure the goal was to kill us both."

"You saw the driver?" Mike said.

Alex and I both answered at the same time. "No."

"So how'd you know it was a male?"

I shook my head. "I guess I was using the masculine form. Or maybe I assumed..."

Mike said, "Where'd you first see the vehicle?"

"We were at Billy's Place. I noticed it soon after we left. But we were a few miles onto 95 when I started thinking whoever it was had been following us."

"And what'd you do?"

I shrugged. "Just kept driving. Once I was sure he was following us, we went past..." I wondered how much I needed to tell him. I didn't want him to know where we were going. "We jumped on 295, going east. Of course, the truck's still on our tail. I turned off onto Greenland Road, going back the other way."

"West?"

I nodded. "Grabbed the first road off of that, don't even remember the name."

"Fayal Drive," Mike said.

"Maybe. We ended up in some industrial park, thought we lost him. But apparently not."

Alex said, "We were stopped. I was turned around in my seat, looking the other way. Henry screamed to get out of the car." She reached for the back of her head. "I barely made it out."

Her eyes filled with tears. "I wasn't sure if you got out of it in time."

We both had our eyes on each other for a moment. Other than the beeping and the medical staff outside the room, we were all quiet.

"The car was crushed like an accordion," Mike said. "It was burning when Jax Fire showed up. I'm honestly surprised to see you both alive."

Alex nodded. "The truck came out of nowhere."

Mike stuck his hand in his pocket and pulled out another toothpick. "Nobody thought to get a plate?" He looked at Billy.

Billy said, "I wasn't there."

Mike said, "Walsh, didn't you think to get the plate before you ran away, left Alex for dead?"

Mike and I kept a stare on each other for what felt like five minutes.

But I knew he was right. If I'd only gotten the plate.

"We tried to," Alex said. "Who would've expected—" She stopped, closing her eyes.

Billy said, "What if it was the same kid who came in looking for you last night?"

Mike pulled the toothpick from his mouth and said to Billy, "What *kid*?"

I was hoping that didn't come up. But it was too late.

Billy had no choice. He had to go ahead and tell Mike about the young man who'd stopped at his restaurant looking for me.

Mike said to Billy, "Would you mind coming down to head-quarters? We'll run you through some visuals, see if we can come up with someone who matches this person's description."

Billy shrugged, nodding. "Sure, I can do that."

I said, "But we have no idea if it's the same person."

Mike said to me, "You got a better lead?"

Chapter 11

I LEANED FORWARD FROM the back seat of Billy's car, resting my hand on Alex's shoulder. She hadn't said a word since we left the hospital.

I said, "Are you okay?"

She directed her gaze at me, and I could see by the look on her face she'd been holding something back. "I think we should have been straight with Mike. I wish we gave him the details he needs."

"What'd I leave out?" I said. "I told him all he needed to know."

"He wanted to know what we were doing down there. Maybe we should have told him we were on our way to Losco Park."

"What good would *that* do?" I said. "He doesn't need to know my business."

Billy glanced back at me. "I don't know. Maybe she's right. Would it really hurt to tell him more? I'm sure you want to find whoever it was that almost killed you?"

I leaned against the back seat, looking out the passenger-side window. "I don't need the friction right now. I know how Mike is. He won't make things easy. Not when we're going up against the sheriff's office once again."

Billy had his eyes back on the road. "I'm thinking about, well... Don't forget, I got a personal invite to go see him at headquarters. What am I supposed to say when he starts digging for information? You know he's going to ask what else I know. He knows I picked you up, and that we're all friends. I think there's going to be pressure put on me to come clean with him. And I'm not sure I want to be the one lying to the cops."

"Leaving things out isn't the same as lying," I said.

Alex said, "Billy's right. It's not fair that he—"

"Mike's not dumb, although sometimes I have to wonder. But I can almost guarantee you he knows I didn't give him the whole story. And that's exactly why he's asked Billy down there." I leaned forward again and said to Billy, "It's not like you'll be under oath."

Alex said, "Mike's got a pretty powerful BS detector. I think trying to keep him in the dark might turn out to be to our detriment."

The three of us were quiet for the last couple of miles, until Billy drove into Alex's driveway. I pushed open the door before

78

he turned off the engine, getting out to help Alex out from the passenger seat. I held out my hand for her to hold on to.

"I'm not crippled," she said, ignoring my gesture. She walked up the driveway toward her house and stopped at her Jeep, looking back at me and Billy with a concerned look on her face. "I don't hear Raz." She looked in her Jeep and walked past it, stopping again at the bottom steps to her porch. "I hope someone has my keys?"

I reached into my pocket and followed after her, the keys in my hand.

She took them, and said, "I left my Glock in the—"

"I'll get it," I said, going back to the car. I reached inside and took her gun out from the glove box.

Alex said, "Henry?"

She'd started backing away from her door and down the steps.

"What is it?" I said, glancing at Billy as we started toward her.

She took the Glock from me and, with her voice hushed, said, "My door... it's open."

I went up the steps and stopped at the open door, looking back at Billy running to his car. He popped open the trunk and took out the old Sig Sauer .45 he'd kept back there for as long as I'd known him.

I waited, looking at Alex and Billy—both armed—and grabbed a shovel that had been leaning against the house.

"Raz was home this whole time?" I said.

Alex nodded, her face as white as it had been when we took her to the hospital.

"I'm sure he's all right," I said. But my heart raced.

I pushed open the door, holding the shovel in one hand.

Alex was behind me. "Oh, Raz... please be all right."

We walked inside, being careful with each step, but Alex's house was old. It was hard to walk without a creak from the hardwood floor.

I gripped the shovel with both hands, holding it like a baseball bat, and peeked into the empty kitchen. I continued down the hall to the TV room on the right.

"Oh no," I said, stepping through the doorway.

Alex gasped, raising the Glock up in front of her.

The couch and love seat were both tipped over, as was Alex's desk. Her TV was still on the wall, but the screen was shattered. The coffee table was broken in half, like someone had jumped on it, and the walls were spray-painted red.

We all looked across the room where someone had written on the wall with the paint, in big, dripping red letters:

NEXT TIME YOU WILL NOT SURVIVE!!!

Alex pushed past me and walked up to the wall, staring at it. She touched the paint, which had already dried, then ran from the room.

I heard running footsteps on the stairs above my head.

Billy had his Sig Sauer .45 by his side and tried to pull open a closet door. But it was locked.

"Her gun safe," I said. "You'll never get it open." I left the room and ran after Alex, up the stairs.

But she was in the hall, on the top step, looking down at me with her finger up, pointing toward her bedroom. She put her finger in front of her lips, then turned for her room.

I slowly took each step, trying to be quiet.

But she'd gone into her bedroom and yelled as I hit the top step.

"Raz!"

I dropped the shovel and ran in after her.

Alex was crouched on the floor, looking under her bed. "You okay, boy? Come on, Raz. It's okay. You can come out."

I checked her closet and went into her bathroom, pulling back the shower curtain to make sure nobody was there.

The house appeared to be empty.

I hurried out to Alex, down on her stomach now, trying to coax Raz out from his hiding spot. "Come on out, Raz. It's okay now." She turned to me with tears in her eyes. "He's shaking like a leaf."

I crouched down next to her and saw Raz's scared, glowing eyes looking at us from under the bed. "Is he okay?"

Alex didn't answer, crawling under the bed with her legs sticking out. "Come on, Raz. It's all right now."

Finally, he crawled out from under. Alex wrapped her arms around him, pulling his head against her chest. The poor dog's body shook, and he moved his legs, trying to get as close to Alex as he could.

Billy walked into the room. "Is he okay?"

Alex nodded. "I think so."

"I looked everywhere," he said. "Whoever did this is long gone."

I crawled over to Alex and Raz, petting his head. "You're a good dog, Raz."

Chapter 12

I HAD A SLEEPLESS night on Alex's couch, but all that mattered to me was that Alex could at least get some much-needed rest. I got up and went into the kitchen, looking out the bay window over her sink, at the orange clouds forming over the rising sun.

I couldn't help but wonder if I knew what I was doing, or if solving Lance Moreau's murder was nothing more than luck. There was no doubt it was part of it, but I couldn't help but wonder if I'd jumped the gun getting my private investigator's license. Maybe it'd been too long since my detective training. Maybe my lack of experience was starting to show.

The thing I hadn't expected was putting the life of someone I cared about in danger.

But one thing had become clear: someone had something to hide and was going to do whatever was necessary to keep me and Alex from figuring out exactly what it was.

I turned from the sink with the sound of Raz's thick nails clicking on the floor. He came over to me, tail wagging.

I crouched down to pet him, rubbing his head with both hands. "Good boy, Raz. You're a good dog."

Alex stepped in through the doorway, with a yawn. "Did you get any sleep?"

I shrugged, still dressed in the clothes I'd worn the day before.

She walked to the refrigerator and pulled out a container of orange juice, pouring herself a glass with her back to me. I could hear each gulp, finishing the juice like she hadn't had a drink in days.

"You okay?" I said.

"Sorry, I couldn't talk, I was so thirsty." She pulled out another glass and filled it, holding it toward me. "Here."

I took the glass but left it on the counter. "I wasn't sure if I should bring you breakfast. You sure you don't want to stay in bed?"

She shook her head, then touched the back of her head. "I think it hurts more than it did yesterday." She put her empty glass in the sink and looked out the window. "Pretty sky," she said, then faced me. "Mike called."

"This morning?"

"Last night," she said.

"To check in, see how you were doing?"

She took a moment before she answered, slowly shaking her head. "I had to tell him the truth, Henry. I'm sorry. It's—"

"It's okay," I said. "I figured you were going to. I mean, I know you didn't have a choice. It's not like he was going to just leave it alone at this point. Not when you're the one who was hurt." I walked to the pub-height table under the window and sat on one of the stools. "Mike's going to do whatever he has to, to keep you safe. I can't argue with that."

Alex appeared to force a smile, but it seemed to be a bit of a challenge. "I'm sorry. But at least now that the cat's out of the bag, you don't have to hide the fact you're investigating the case."

"I hope he's not going to go out of his way to stop me."

"He wouldn't," she said.

"And after all that's happened so far, I'd have to say whatever reason Angela had for believing John's death wasn't an accident... she seemed to've hit the nail on the head."

Alex kneeled next to Raz, running her hand over his big head. I could sense the doubt in her expression. "The thing is, can we really say this is all connected to John Thompson's death? I'm... I'm not sure. I'm sorry, but—"

"Is this coming from you?" I said. "Or is this just what Mike said? Because, I mean, come on, Alex. What else could it be? You really think it's all random?"

"I didn't say it was random. And neither did Mike. But he doesn't think we should jump to any conclusions yet. He actually agreed to help, but he'd need evidence from you. Especially considering how bad it could look for the sheriff's office."

"He's more interested in protecting the sheriff's office than finding the truth?"

"No. But he's also not in a position to put his neck on the line without having something more he can run with. A truck we can't find, and someone ransacking my home isn't enough. It's not, Henry."

Raz came and sat down at my feet. "I was awake all night, trying to think of who else would do something like this. Since Lance's investigation, all I've had are small-time clients with mostly minor cases. I was thinking about one, this guy, George Dawson. It took me a month to prove he was cheating on his wife. He did say something about getting revenge on me." I said, "And then there was that workers' comp case. The meathead I followed was lifting weights in the gym three hours a day but wouldn't go back to work. But there's no way he'd know I was the one watching him."

Alex said, "But there is a chance someone else—"

"You weren't involved in any of those cases. And I can't think of anybody who'd..." I stopped mid-sentence and stood from the stool. "It could be someone—the person who broke in here—is only going after you because they know what it would do to me, if something were ever to happen to you."

Alex was watching me, staring into my eyes.

We were both quiet.

She went to the stove and grabbed the teapot, filling it with water. "What about your boat? Shouldn't we go check on it?"

"Billy went by the marina last night." I smiled. "He said it was trashed, but I'm not sure it was trashed any more than it normally is."

Alex let out a laugh. She stood at the sink, looking out the window.

I looked at the back of her head, shaved, where they'd given her the stitches. She'd removed the bandage. "That'll itch when your hair grows back," I said. "I need to go by Thompson Insurance."

"Now?"

"Soon," I said. "I'm going to talk to Kayla. She's the one who worked alongside John for a few years and must know plenty about whatever was going on in his life." I drank the orange juice from the glass on the counter. "I'm going to stop by the boat, get cleaned up and out of these clothes. I know you're supposed to be resting, but I'm not sure I want to leave you here alone."

"I'm fine," Alex said. "I can go with you. But I can't leave Raz home alone. No way."

"Billy said he'd watch Raz, if you want."

"At the restaurant?"

"He said Raz can have the whole upstairs to himself, instead of—"

My phone rang. I pulled it from my pocket. "Speak of the devil."

It was Billy.

I answered, "Morning."

"Oh good, you're up. Listen. Chloe got that kid's phone number."

"What kid?"

"The one who came in the restaurant looking for you. He returned late last night, after I got back from the sheriff's office. I asked for his number, but he refused to give it to me. I asked if he wanted a drink, hoping I'd be able to check his ID and get his name, but he said no. So, I got Chloe to talk to him, make him think she was interested."

I said, "And she got his number?"

"Of course she did. And also his name: Nate Ryan."

"Nate Ryan?" I said, eyeing Alex. "That's John Thompson's stepson, from John's second marriage."

Chapter 13

I DIALED NATE RYAN's phone number at least seven times on the ride over to Thompson Insurance, but each call went to a standard message, saying the caller was not available.

"Maybe he made it up," Alex said from the passenger seat of her Jeep. "He could've given Chloe a number that wasn't even his."

"The way Billy said it, the kid thought he was giving an attractive young bartender his phone number. She didn't tell him it was for me. Any normal kid his age would be crazy not to give Chloe the correct phone number."

We parked in front of the building for Thompson Insurance, and Alex's phone rang on our way toward the entrance.

"It's Mike," she said, answering the call. "Hey, Mike." She listened. "Really? Where?" She nodded into the phone. "Yes, it had a black bull bar on the front of it." She was quiet for a moment. "Oh, okay. Thanks, Mike. I appreciate the call." She tapped the screen on her phone and stuck it in her pocket.

"What'd he say?" I said, reaching for the door at the building's entrance.

"Someone in the industrial park saw the white truck speeding past their building at a pretty good clip, right around the time of our accident. He said the truck almost hit the man's car as he was pulling out of his parking space."

I pulled on the glass door and let Alex in ahead of me. "But no plate or anything else? I'm not sure it gives us much more."

"I think he wanted me to know he's involved, and taking it seriously."

We walked up to the security guard at the desk. I said to Alex, "But isn't that his job? To take a crime seriously?"

The security guard appeared to recognize us from our first visit. "Thompson Insurance?" he said, sliding the clipboard across the desk. "You know the drill."

• • • • • • • • • •

We got off the elevator onto the twelfth floor and through the glass doors into the Thompson Insurance reception area. I asked the young woman behind the desk for Kayla Morton.

"I'm sorry," she said. "Kayla's not here today."

I said, "Is she sick?"

She didn't exactly answer. "Did you have an appointment with her?"

"I talked to her last night. She knew we were coming in to meet with her."

The young woman looked at her computer. "Would you like me to see if someone else is available to help you?"

I glanced at Alex and nodded at the young woman. "Is Angela here?"

"I can see if she's available." She put the phone up to her ear and dialed, waiting. After a moment, she finally said, "Oh, hi, Mrs. Thompson. There's a gentleman out here who had an appointment to see Kayla. But..." She paused, then covered the mouthpiece on the handset. "What is your name, sir?"

"Tell her it's Henry and Alex."

The woman moved her hand from the phone. "Henry and Alex?" She nodded, listening to Angela on the other end. "Okay, sure thing. I'll tell him." She placed the phone on the base and pointed toward the chairs, along the wall behind us. "Have a seat. Mrs. Thompson will be right with you."

Alex and I sat, and at least fifteen minutes had gone by until Angela finally stuck her head out from the open door to the offices. "Forgive me for the wait," she said, holding open the door for us to walk in ahead of her.

She stepped past us, and we followed her down the hall, but she had stopped to look at Alex. "What happened to your head?"

I said, "We'll tell you all about it."

We continued down the hall and into a large office, with walls made of mostly glass. The view overlooked the St. Johns.

And considering I lived right *on* the St. Johns, I didn't have the same view as one from twelve stories above.

Angela sat behind her desk and gestured for me and Alex to sit in the two chairs across from her. She leaned forward as we sat, folding her hands in front of her. She said, "So, what can I do for you?"

I said, "Well, we're actually here to meet with Kayla."

"Oh," Angela said. She appeared surprised. "How come I didn't hear anything about this *meeting*?"

"I didn't think it mattered. Do you prefer I tell you everyone I'm going to be talking to?" I knew, as soon as the words left my mouth, I had given Angela an attitude, although I didn't mean to.

Angela put up her hands in defense. "It was *just* a question."

We had our eyes on each other for a moment. "I'm sorry," I said. "It's been a long twenty-four hours." I turned toward the open door. "So, where *is* Kayla?"

"Well, I'm actually upset myself. I don't like the idea Kayla tells you to meet her here, but doesn't reach out to you when she decides she won't be coming in." Angela sighed. "A little common courtesy goes a long way, but this younger generation..."

"It certainly would've saved us a trip," I said.

Angela cracked a slight grin. "Well, I guess now you're stuck spending more time with me." She straightened out a handful of papers on her desk and moved them to a small table behind her, then looked at Alex. "So, can you tell me what happened to your head?"

Alex said to me, "Go ahead, you can tell her."

"Okay," I said, leaning forward on the chair. "As I'd said, the last twenty-four hours have been something. It all started with someone trying to kill us."

Angela's eyes opened wide. "Someone tried to kill you? Are you serious?"

I said, "Do you know anyone who drives a white Ford pick-up truck?"

Angela shook her head. "I don't think so. No."

"Because whoever drives it—a Ford F-250—drove head-on toward me and Alex and tried to crush us both."

Angela said, "You mean, on purpose?"

"I'd say so. No reason to think otherwise. But, right now, we have no idea who could've been behind the wheel. My car was destroyed, but luckily we both made it out alive."

Angela said to Alex, "So that's how you got the wound on the back of your head?"

"Henry and I both got out before the truck made impact."

"We barely escaped," I said, glancing at Alex.

Alex said, "I'm not even sure where I hit my head. Henry found me, barely conscious."

Angela said, "I guess you weren't kidding when you said it was a long twenty-four hours?"

"It didn't end there," I said. "But I wish it did."

"Oh no," Angela said, waiting for the rest of the story.

I said, "Somebody broke into Alex's house and tore the place apart."

Angela gasped. "Did they take anything?"

"They turned over furniture, broke my TV and my coffee table, plus scared the crap out of my dog."

"They spray-painted a threat on her wall," I said.

"I assume you called the sheriff's office?" Angela said.

Alex nodded but didn't say much else about it.

Angela cleared her throat, leaning back in her chair. "Do you believe this has something to do with the investigation?"

"Funny," I said. "I was thinking I should ask you the same question. Because I can't stop wondering what you're not telling me. I'm not saying you're being dishonest with me, but the fact you'd hire a private investigator because your ex-husband wasn't wearing a bicycle helmet doesn't make a lot of sense."

"I understand your frustration," Angela said. "But I—"

"It's not just frustration," I said. "You're putting lives in danger. *Our* lives. And something tells me there's a reason you're leaving us in the dark like this." I stood up from the chair and leaned with my hands on the desk, looking down at her. "All I'm asking is for you to be honest with me."

Angela tried to get away from my stare, but I wouldn't let her.

"Angela? Please..."

"Okay, listen. I'm telling you the truth. I don't know what else there was. But okay. The thing is, I believe John was up to something. Something was wrong, up until the day he died. But I have no idea what it was. I know there was something."

I said, "You don't know what you don't know? Is that what you're telling me?"

Alex said, "Can't you at least be a little more specific?"

Angela got up from her chair and reached into a small refrigerator behind her desk. She reached in for three bottles of water and placed two on the desk for me and Alex. She opened the third one herself and took a sip.

She twisted the top back on and pushed the bottle aside. "The truth is, we had quite a rough patch here for a while. Our business. Thompson Insurance hadn't been doing very well, and it caused some serious stress between me and John."

"Recently?" I said.

She nodded. "You could say that."

"So maybe that's why your brother-in-law—"

"Eric? What did he say?" She shook her head. "I should have warned you: take whatever comes out of his mouth with a grain of salt."

"He said you and John were at each other's throats. To be honest, when I asked him if there was anyone John had any conflicts with, you know who he said?"

Angela said, "I can only guess. Did he say it was *me*?"

"I guess that's no surprise?" I said. "Can you tell us why he would say that?"

"You know what's funny about Eric saying I was the one John had conflicts with? If it wasn't for me, John would've thrown Eric out of this company a long time ago. I'm the only reason he still has a job here."

Chapter 14

I WAS DRIVING ALEX'S Jeep, on our way to Billy's, when a number showed up on my phone I recognized right away, because I'd been calling it all afternoon.

I answered, "Walsh Investigations."

A young man's voice was on the other end. "Did you say *Walsh Investigations*?"

"That's right," I said. "Is there something I can help you with?"

"I had a few missed calls from this number today."

"Is this Nate?" I said.

The young man paused. "Yeah. Are you the one who's been calling me?"

"Haven't you been looking for me?" I said.

I felt like we were both playing a bit of a game.

Nate said, "How'd you get my number?"

"I'm a private investigator," I said. "I have my ways." I wasn't about to get Chloe in any kind of trouble for giving me the kid's number.

"Where are you?" I said.

"At the St. Johns Town Center."

I crossed lanes, heading for the upcoming exit. "I'll be there in five minutes."

"Oh, okay, uh..."

"Where are you?" I said.

"By the fountain, at one of the tables."

"I'll find you."

• • • ◉ • ◉ • • •

Alex and I walked across the parking lot at the St. Johns Town Center and passed a pond with a small, bubbling fountain in the middle. A sign read Please Do Not Feed the Turtles. We continued toward the courtyard area with dozens of tables with umbrellas and mostly empty chairs. I spotted a young man with light, almost blond hair, sitting alone. He was tall and appeared quite thin, like a full-grown boy.

He stood from the table when he spotted us walking toward him. "Mr. Walsh?"

"Henry," I said, about to shake his hand, but he had a bandage on the back of it. Not to mention some sort of a rash that covered the back of his arm. "You must be Nate?" I introduced him to Alex, and he stared back at her, without saying a word for a handful of seconds.

"Nate?" I said. "Are you okay?"

As if he'd snapped himself from a trance, he stammered, "Huh? Oh... yes. I'm sorry, it's not, it's..." He looked toward the fountain, then back at Alex. "For a second, you reminded me of someone else."

Alex had a look on her face like she didn't know how to react.

The three of us sat at the table.

I said, "Who does she remind you of?"

Nate sipped from a tall red cup, with Coca-Cola written up the side. "Don't take this the wrong way, or I hope it doesn't sound weird, but"—he looked at Alex—"you look a little like my mom."

Alex raised her eyebrows. "Your mom? Theresa Thompson?"

Nate Nodded. "Theresa *Ryan*."

I said, "Isn't her last name Thompson?"

"Technically, er... legally, yes. She's Theresa Thompson. But to me and the rest of my family, she's Theresa Ryan."

Alex gave me a look out of the corner of her eye.

Nate said, "She passed away."

"We know all about your mother," I said.

"You know about her because you're investigating John's death?"

"Yes," I said, "although let me clarify that I know a *little* about your mother. Not as much as I should."

Nate leaned over the table and sipped his drink from the straw, without using his hands.

"I'm sorry about your stepfather," I said.

Nate made a face, twisted like I'd said something foolish. "My stepfather?" He shook his head. "John's not my stepfather. He never really was, as far as I was concerned. And especially after my mother died. He's nothing to me. I don't consider him my stepfather, or anything like that."

I moved in closer to the table, leaning on my arm. "So how'd you know about me?" I said. "Who told you I was investigating John's death?"

Nate appeared hesitant, like he wasn't sure he should answer. "You talked to a friend of mine who bartends. She said you'd gone in there asking questions."

"Lydia?" I said.

He nodded.

"I didn't know you were a friend of hers. And, well, she doesn't seem to have the same bad feelings as you seem to about your—about John. In fact, she was quite upset about what happened to him. I'm surprised she didn't mention you."

"Well, it's not like we're great friends or anything. But I did see her the other night, and she mentioned a private eye stopped in when she was behind the bar. She had your card." Nate smiled. "She said you broke her boyfriend's nose."

"Her boyfriend? Brian Mason is her boyfriend?"

Nate nodded. "Yeah. And he owns the place."

"I know that. But she never mentioned he was her boyfriend."

"I don't know for sure," Nate said. "It's one of those things. Maybe they're not really together much anymore. I didn't ask."

"Do you know him?" I said.

"Brian?" Nate nodded. "He used to come over to the house when I was little, but my mom didn't like me being around him. Mr. Mason was at our house all the time, and he'd bring Brian, try to get us to be friends. The kid would always break my toys."

Alex said, "So it sounds like you and Brian were never really friends?"

Nate shook his head and leaned back in his chair. "I don't think my mother liked Roy a whole lot, either. I remember the two of them having arguments about it."

"Roy and your mom?"

"No, I meant John and my mom. She didn't like that Roy was always at the house."

"That's interesting," I said.

"Is it?" Nate pulled the plastic cover off his drink and sipped from the cup. His mouth filled with ice cubes, and he chewed them, taking a few moments before he spoke. "You know, I wanted to be a cop when I was younger. Actually, I applied, but my background..." He took another mouthful of ice.

I said, "What *about* your background?"

He chewed what was in his mouth, crunching the ice between his teeth. "I smoked a lot of pot in my teens. Got caught a couple of times, too. So it's on my permanent record. I was doing quite a bit of drinking at one point, and got into a little trouble with that, too. So I thought, if I can't be a cop... maybe I could be a private investigator."

I wondered if I had it all wrong about why this young man had been looking for me.

I said, "That's not actually why you called me, is it?"

Nate paused, then said, "Yes and no. Well, what got me thinking about it is I've already been doing some investigating lately. I'm trying to find out why I never got any money when my mom died. I was told I had something coming, but I had to wait until I was twenty-one. Then my aunt..." He turned to Alex. "I used to live with my aunt. And she said John kept all the money after my mom died, and that some of it belonged to me."

I leaned forward on the table. "You believe John owed you money?"

Nate nodded. "He still does. Even if he's dead." He cleared his throat. "Is that something you might be able to help me with? If I got the money, I could pay you."

With my elbow resting on the table I ran my hand over my face. "Do you know how this could look?" I said. "I mean, we don't know exactly what happened to John and how he died. But, with you telling me—or anyone else you've told—that he owes you money..."

"I've actually been calling this girl at John's office. I guess she was his assistant or something. I called to see if she could help me get my hands on the life insurance policy."

Alex said, "Your mother's policy?"

Nate nodded. "Yeah, but she never returned my calls. I called her at least a dozen times. So a couple of nights ago, I found out where she lived and went to her apartment. And as I walked up to her place, thinking I'd knock on her door and introduce myself..." He was quiet for a moment. "This white truck drove past me. I swear the guy driving it almost hit me."

I sat up straight in my seat and saw Alex staring back at me. "A white truck? What kind of a white truck?"

"I don't know. F-250, I think." He looked from me to Alex. "Why do you both look so surprised? I'm not sure why I even mentioned it..."

"Anything you remember about it? Any scratches or dents or anything at all that'd make it stand out?"

Nate nodded. "Had one of those big metal bars on the front. I don't remember what you call 'em."

I said, "A bull bar?"

"Yeah, that's it. A bull bar."

Chapter 15

IT DIDN'T TAKE MUCH convincing for me to get Nate to come with us over to Kayla's apartment. I assumed she'd be home, considering she'd called in sick. And Nate already knew where she lived. He seemed too happy to join us, even at one point saying how cool it was for him to be working side by side with a real private investigator.

I said to Nate, "So you never spoke with Kayla the night you were at her apartment?"

"No, sir," he said.

"And how come you never spoke to John about the money?"

Nate deadpanned. "Because he's dead."

I watched him in the mirror, waiting for his expression to say he was being a smart-ass. But he just sat there in the back seat of the Jeep, like he meant nothing by it. I wondered if maybe the young man's brain simply hadn't fully developed. "What I meant was, it sounds like you've known about this money or the insurance policy, for a little while now, right? Why didn't you talk to John sooner?"

Nate shrugged. "Well, I hadn't talked to him in a long time. Probably a few years. I assume you can tell... it's not like we were ever close."

"And what about Michelle?" I said. "John's widow? I understand she was your nanny, huh?" I gave him a quick look over my shoulder. "I was a little surprised to hear that after doing the math. Don't take this personally, but I'm thinking you must've been on the older side for having a nanny?"

I watched Nate through the mirror, rolling his eyes.

"My mom hired her when I was younger, because she used to travel for work. Michelle took care of me, made sure I had someone around. It was me and my mom, so..."

"Where was John?" I said.

"Oh, she hired Michelle before she met him."

"But it sounds like Michelle was still around, even as you got older?"

I wasn't sure by the look on Nate's face, he was enjoying the questioning.

"It wasn't up to me," he said. "I didn't pay her. But she did other stuff around the house, too, like cleaning and doing the shopping. And she'd pick me up from school or whatever else they told her to do. My mom wanted to get rid of her at one point, but John was around by then, and he insisted they keep her." Nate laughed. "I guess now we know the reason why."

I glanced over at Alex, shaking her head.

We pulled into the parking lot of the Jax, a fancy-looking, modern apartment complex with a sign at the entrance that said they had two pools and tennis courts and a movie theater for residents only. The landscaping was nice enough, with big flowering trees and grass so green it almost looked fake.

Nate walked ahead of us to Kayla's building and stopped at the curb, pointed to the street along the sidewalk. "This is where I saw the truck. It was right there."

I said, "But you didn't look to see who was inside?"

"The windows were tinted," he said. "It was parked, and I don't think the engine was running. There's a chance nobody was in it."

We continued toward the entrance to the building, but the plate-glass door was locked. A man was on his way out and held the door to let us in. The lobby had marble floors with large potted plants in every corner, the bright white walls decorated with framed artwork, and a TV hung on the wall in front of a seating area with a leather couch and two matching chairs.

We took the elevator up to the seventh floor, the three of us mostly quiet on the ride up. The doors slid open, and Nate turned left without hesitation, continuing down the hall until we stopped at apartment number 7203.

I leaned close to the door to listen, but it was quiet on the other side. I knocked.

"What if she really *is* sick?" Alex said, making a face like she wouldn't enjoy the germs.

I turned toward her, but before I responded, the door opened.

Kayla stood in the doorway, looking from me to Alex and then fixing her gaze on Nate. "What, what's going on? Why are you all..." She kept her hand on the doorknob, like she was getting ready to pull it closed.

"You missed our meeting today, so I thought we should come make sure you're okay."

Kayla wasn't wearing pajamas or whatever she might've lounged around in if she were actually sick. In fact, she didn't look like someone who had just rolled out of bed or off the couch. She was dressed, wearing makeup, and I could smell her flowery perfume.

"I'm sorry I didn't let you know. I-I'm not feeling well today. I should have called you."

"You look all right for someone who's sick," I said.

"Well, it's not that I'm actually sick. Or, I'm not *ill*, I should say. It's... things have been really stressful at the office. I needed a day to myself to step away from it all." Her gaze shifted to Nate. "Are you... are you *Nate*?"

Nate grinned, stepping forward between me and Alex. "I didn't know if you'd recognize me. It's been a long time."

Her face turned red. "I almost didn't recognize you. You were just a little kid last time I saw you." She smiled. "You've grown quite a bit." But the smile left her face. "I'm really sorry that you... that I haven't returned your calls. I should have..."

She paused, looking from Nate to me and Alex. "Why are you all together, at my apartment?"

I said, "Well, we were supposed to talk. So I thought we'd come by and see if you were up to it. I'd also like to know if you know the person who owns the white Ford pickup truck that was parked outside your building recently?"

Kayla stared back at me, shaking her head. "A what? A white pickup? I have no idea. I'm not even sure I know *anyone* who drives a truck."

I had a feeling Alex needed to get off her feet. She had already completely ignored the doctor's orders to rest, which was, of course, clearly my fault. I said to Kayla, "Would it be all right if we came inside?"

Kayla took a moment to answer. "Uh, actually, I'm—"

"Don't worry," I said. "We won't take much of your time. I know you're home, hoping to relax, which I completely understand, but..."

Kayla looked into her apartment. "It's, well, the place is a mess." She paused. "How about if we go outside? We can go down to the pool area? There's nobody down there now, and we can talk if you'd like?"

I said, "If you saw my place, you'd know a little mess won't bother me. And to be honest, the damage done to Alex's house last night... I can't speak for Nate, but I think we're all used to a mess right now."

Kayla said to Alex, "What happened to your house?"

"We'll get into that later," I said.

Kayla stepped out and pulled the door closed. For whatever reason—maybe it really was a mess—she wasn't going to let us inside. "Come on, it's a nice area down there."

• • • • • • • • • •

The four of us sat at a table by the pool, under the pergola. There was a large wood-paddled fan spinning above our heads, which did a decent job of moving the warm fall air.

Although she'd said there'd be nobody at the pool, there were plenty of kids swimming. Their moms or nannies or whatever responsible adult, who was supposed to keep them from drowning, sat around the edge in lounge chairs. There were no lifeguards.

A couple of the women had their heads in their phones. I couldn't say for sure if they had kids with them or not.

Kayla sat across from me, with Nate and Alex on either side of her. She said, "I'd appreciate it if you didn't tell Angela you saw me today."

I grinned. "Because you're sick and in bed?" I nodded. "Yeah, no worries."

Kayla faced Alex. "Are you going to tell me what happened to your house?"

"Are you going to tell us who was driving the white truck?" I said. I wasn't sure if she knew or not, but I wasn't going to let her off that easy, either.

"I swear, I don't know who owns a white truck. Like I said, I can't think of anyone who owns a truck, period."

"Is it really just a coincidence the same vehicle crashed into us yesterday, and tried to kill me and Alex?"

Kayla gasped, placing her small hands over her mouth. "Someone tried to *kill* you? Is that what happened to the back of your head? You're both okay?"

"They had to stitch her up," I said. "But that's only because we were both lucky to get out. It could've been worse."

Kayla's eyes were wide open, staring at us both, with a look of disbelief on her face.

Alex said, "We got home from the hospital, and my place was trashed."

"Do you think it has to do with John?" Kayla said.

"I'd be surprised if it doesn't," I said.

"And you think the same person trashed your house?"

"Without a doubt," I said. "Whoever it was made it pretty clear with the warning they spray-painted on her wall." I leaned forward with my arms folded on the table. "Would you like to think a little harder, make sure you can't think of any reason the same white truck would be outside your apartment building?"

Kayla shook her head. "I'm telling you the truth. I have no idea who it could've..." She paused. "Are you sure it's the same truck? I mean, there are *lots* of pickup trucks in Florida, in case you haven't noticed?"

"I thought of that. Of course. But this one had a distinct feature—"

Kayla said, "But who saw it? How do you know it was—"

"I saw it," Nate said.

I wasn't going to tell her it was him, but he had a look on his face, like he *wanted* her to know he was the one who saw it.

Kayla cocked her head, staring at Nate. "When were you at my apartment?"

I said, "Nate wants you to help him with this insurance situation. And when you didn't return his calls, he came looking for you. He was doing his own investigative work." I gave him a grin, trying to help him out, because I could see in Kayla's eyes, she didn't like what she'd heard.

She held her gaze on Nate. "*Investigative work?* It sounds to me like he's stalking me!" She pushed her chair out and stood from the table.

I couldn't help but think she was being a bit dramatic.

I got up, trying to stop Kayla from walking away before I'd gotten much of anything out of her. "Kayla, wait a minute. I don't think Nate was stalking you. Take a deep breath, okay? He needs your help. If you could—"

"I'm sorry," she said. "I find it a little creepy, knowing someone was outside my apartment looking for me. I live alone, you know. I don't want some man showing up at my apartment uninvited." She stared at Nate. "Do you understand where I'm coming from?"

111

Nate said, "It wasn't like that at all. I'm sorry if you... I was hoping you would help me. You wouldn't return my calls."

Kayla shook her head. "I can't help you, Nate. I'm sorry." She started to walk away.

"Kayla, wait a minute," I said. "Please."

She stopped and stood with her arms folded. Waiting.

I said to Nate, "How much money are we talking about here?"

"My mom's policy?" He shrugged. "I've never actually seen it myself, but my aunt told me John got two million dollars when my mom died. And I was supposed to see a portion of it when I turned twenty-one."

"And how old are you now?" Alex said.

"Almost twenty-two."

Chapter 16

ROY MASON LIVED A block west of Riverfront Park in San Marco in a long, sprawling ranch with off-white stucco siding and a Spanish-style roof. He didn't live right on the St. Johns, but it was close enough, the way you could see it through the trees, driving up his driveway.

I pulled Alex's Jeep up toward his house and parked in front of the middle door of a three-car garage. The first door to my left was wide open, and I could see the rear end of what looked like an antique pickup truck painted mint green. CHEVRO-LET was painted on the raised white lettering across the tail-gate.

I stepped out of the Jeep and to the garage, looking in at the truck. The hood was open. "Hello? Anybody here?"

Roy Mason poked his head out from under the hood, holding a work light in his hand, hung from a black cord from the rafters. "Yes? " He walked toward me, wiping his hands on a red rag. "Can I help you?" He continued toward me and stepped out from the garage. With his chin raised and his lower jaw protruding, he squinted, looking down at me over his nose. "I know you," he said. "You're that, uh... it's Henry, is that right? The PI?"

I nodded. "Yes, sir."

Even though age appeared to be catching up to Roy with his cropped white hair and receding hairline, he was built like a lumberjack. He had big shoulders, powerful-looking hands, and a square jaw to go with them. His tanned face was covered in white stubble. "Now, I try not to get involved in my boy's business, all right? But I understand you hit him. A sucker punch." He folded the red rag over and stuffed it in his back pocket. "Broke his nose. Did you know that?"

"I believe your son's got his story mixed up," I said. "I was defending myself. He's the one who came after me in the parking lot and—"

"The way he tells it, he was doing you a courtesy, bringing you the keys you'd left on the bar after a few too many drinks. Said you hit him with a sucker punch—a coward punch—coldcocked him when he wasn't expecting it."

I said, "I'm sorry, but that's not at all what happened."

Roy kept his stare on me for a moment, then glanced back into the garage. "Like I said, I don't get involved in my boy's business unless I have to. I'm sure the time'll come, you two can hash it out." He ran his tongue along the inside of his lower lip and stepped past me, shooting a stream of brown spit into the flower bed by the garage.

"I didn't come here to talk about what happened between me and your son," I said.

Roy paused before he answered. "If it's got to do with John's death, then I've said all I'm going to say. Sheriff's office concluded their investigation. And as far as I'm concerned, there's nothing left to discuss."

Roy took a step into the garage with a slight limp as he walked back to the front of his truck. He pulled a wrench from his pocket and ducked his head under the hood.

I followed him in and leaned with one hand on the top of the driver's-side door. "What year's your truck?"

Roy kept his head down, under the hood. "Nineteen forty-seven Chev-ro-let. Feels like I've been working on her for half my life. Was my old man's, but he let it rot out in a field till he passed away at ninety-four. Finally got my hands on it." He glanced at me from under the hood. "Had a Studebaker out there, too, straight outta the Indiana factory. But my wife at the time—we lived in a smaller house than this one—said either I get rid of one of 'em or she was going to leave." He lifted his head out from under the hood and straightened up. "Been fifteen years since she left." He scratched the top of his head. "Never did get round to fixin' up the Studebaker."

Roy walked over to a wood workbench in front of the truck and placed the wrench inside a toolbox. He grabbed the screwdrivers he had laid out on another red rag on the fender and rolled them up. He put them in the same toolbox, then let the hood down gently, until it clicked.

He excused himself past me and stepped into the driver's side with one foot still on the ground. He turned his ear toward the steering wheel as if listening for something, then turned the key.

At first, the engine didn't sound like it wanted to start. It made a clucking sound, then roared to life. Roy smiled as the engine settled down to a purr. He pulled his left foot into the car and closed the door, hanging his elbow out the window as he backed the truck from the garage.

I watched Roy step out onto the driveway, the truck still running, then come back into the garage. He walked to the workbench and stood with his back to me, closing the top on his toolbox. He hung a pair of pliers up on the pegboard in front of him.

"Roy," I said. "I know you're—"

"Give me a minute," he said, putting his index finger in the air at his shoulder so I could see it. "Can't leave a mess like this laying around."

I looked over at two more cars, parked inside the other part of the garage. One was a black Mercedes and the other—on the far side of the garage—was a Range Rover.

Roy wiped his hands with the rag and folded it over into a neat square. He left it on the workbench, then faced me, leaning back with his arms crossed. "You were saying?"

"I know you and John were good friends, and—"

"Like brothers," he said matter-of-factly.

I gave him a slight nod. "I understand you know his stepson fairly well?"

"Nate?" He nodded. "Haven't seen him in, oh, I don't know... at least a couple years. Hope he's more of a man than he was when I last saw him."

I wasn't sure what Roy meant, but I didn't think there was any significance to it. "Nate came looking for me, because he'd heard I was working for Angela."

Roy cleared his throat. "Just so you and me are on the same page, I want to make sure you understand where I'm coming from with regard to this so-called investigation."

"I do," I said. "I understand. But I also want to make sure you understand I have a job to do, and I intend to see this investigation through to the end. Even if I determine John's death was indeed an accident, then I've still done my job. But I won't allow someone to get in my way because he doesn't believe in what I'm doing."

Roy narrowed his eyes. "But don't you have an obligation to your client to let her know the chances are *real* good there's nothing else you're going to find? And that you're not only wasting time, but also Angela's hard-earned money?"

I shook my head. "I don't believe I'm wasting anything."

Roy let out a strong sigh. "Son, this was a *tragic* accident. But there ain't nothing more to it." He walked past me, and I followed him out to the driveway. He reached into the truck and turned off the engine, pulled out the keys, and dropped them in his front pocket.

"I gotta be honest with you, Roy. I've already got a list of possible suspects. And in fact, the way your son acted has me kind of wondering what it is he's trying to hide."

Roy stuck out his chest. "I'll tell you right now; my boy values those closest to him... and those who're close to me. Are you going to blame him for being suspicious when some stranger goes into his place of business, asking questions about a man my boy's known most of his life?"

I wanted to laugh, but I played it cool. "Sounds to me you're admitting there was more to my run-in with your son than me landing a sucker punch?"

Roy stood still for a moment, then headed toward the stairs leading to his front door. He stopped and turned back to me. "You want to snoop around my house? My businesses? My kid's business? Well, I'll promise you something. The Masons aren't going to just sit there and let you do whatever you want. You keep doing what you're doing, and I suggest you make sure you prepare yourself for whatever may come your way."

I took a step closer to him. He was a big man, but I wasn't afraid of him. We stood face-to-face. I said, "Are you threatening me, Roy?"

Roy didn't move at first, then stepped to the garage and pulled the door closed. He started up the stone-faced steps, leading to his front door, but stopped and turned as he reached the landing. "I'm letting you know where I stand. You can take that for what it is."

Chapter 17

ALEX AND RAZ WERE already waiting for me on the dock at the marina when I got back from Roy Mason's. I'd picked up a pizza, some food for Raz, and a six-pack of a local brew the young man behind the register recommended. It was a perfect fall night. Still warm, but nothing like it had been a few weeks earlier.

By the time I'd settled down in my chair next to Alex, she was on her feet. "I'm sorry," she said. "But I should probably get home."

I stood, looking at the pizza neither of us had touched. "Aren't you going to eat?" I thought for a moment, shaking my head. "I don't think you should go home alone. I wouldn't be able to sleep, knowing you're there and—"

"I can take care of myself," she said. "You know that, don't you?" She crouched down to pet Raz, sleeping on the dock under my chair. "We'll be all right, won't we, Raz?"

"He's still out there," I said. "Whoever he is."

"He, or she," Alex said. "You never know."

I put my beer down on the dock. "I know you can handle yourself. But I think it's smart to, you know, stick by each other. It's not worth the risk right now. Just have a slice of pizza, drink a beer, and hang out. You and Raz can sleep in my bed. I'll sleep up there, on the deck."

"You're going to sleep outside?" She straightened up and cracked a smile. "I don't like the idea of it... come over in the morning, and you're floating facedown in the river." Her expression dropped. "Besides, what makes you think we're safer here? We're out in the open, exposed to anyone who wants to come here, go right on your boat."

I picked up my beer and took a sip. "I'm not sure it's where we are that makes us safer. But wouldn't you say we're better off together at this point? If anything happened to you, I'd never forgive myself. I'm the one who pulled you into this situation."

Alex let out a sigh. "All right," she said, looking down at Raz. "You all right sleeping in Henry's bed?"

Raz kept his head down.

Alex climbed up onto the boat and grabbed a slice of pizza and a beer from the cooler and stayed up there, looking around.

She looked like she was about to say something, but my phone buzzed. "It's Nate," I said, looking at the screen. "A text."

I read it to Alex:

Stopped by River's Edge. Heard Brian is mad. Looking for you.

"You've got to be kidding me," I said.

Alex stepped down from the boat and onto the dock. "That's not good."

"No, it's not. I bet Roy told him I was over there; now the guy's all wound up."

Alex gave me a look. "Was that your intention?"

I finished my beer and grabbed another, twisting the top from the bottle. "I'm not sure what you mean."

"Did you say something to Roy to get Brian wound up? Instigating?"

"Not at all," I said. "He's the one who brought it up, said that Brian said I sucker-punched him. I told him what really happened, although it seemed to me—as would make sense—Roy had no choice but to believe his own son."

Alex said, "Any chance he knows where you live?"

I wondered the same thing myself. "Not many people know I live here, or how to find me." I glanced at Raz, sleeping. "On second thought," I said. "Maybe it doesn't make sense for you and Raz to stay here. But I don't think you should go back to your house, either."

She said, "Are you serious?"

"I don't know. Maybe we call Billy? He'd let you stay there for the night. I don't want to risk it, if this nutjob's planning to track me down."

Alex seemed annoyed. "Didn't you just say, two minutes ago, that we were safer together?"

"I did, but now that—"

"So what you're saying is you don't need me to stick around to help protect *you*? But what, because I'm female, I need *you* to protect *me*?" She laughed, shaking her head.

I said, "You know that's not at all what I'm saying. But if this fool happens to show up—"

"You have no idea if he will," Alex said. "You said yourself, nobody knows you live here."

I turned, looking out at the river.

Alex said, "Why don't you call Nate back?"

I nodded, taking my phone from my pocket. I tapped Nate's number and waited.

He answered on the first ring.

"Henry?"

"Yeah, I saw your text. What's the story? Are you at the bar now?"

Nate said, "At River's Edge. Yeah. Well, sort of."

"Sort of?" I didn't ask for details. "Who told you Brian Mason was looking for me?"

"Uh, Lydia said something about it."

"What'd she say?"

"I told her I'd met you. And that's when she said Brian was ripping mad and said he was going to find you." He was quiet for a moment. "I think she likes you, the way she was talking about you being in there. She likes older men, you know."

The phrase "older men" hung in my head.

"I appreciate the heads-up, Nate. I mean, about Brian. But I can't imagine he's out looking for me at this time of night."

"He's actually still here at the restaurant. He's been drinking."

"But you said in your text he was looking for me."

Nate went quiet again.

"Nate?"

"Yeah, sorry," Nate said. "I was checking my text. I guess I should've been more clear."

"Listen, thanks again for the heads-up, but I can't worry about this right now."

Nate said, "You want me to go inside and talk to Lydia?"

"I thought you said you were already there?"

"I was. But I'm outside now."

I realized what he meant when he said "sort of."

"What are you doing outside?" I said.

"Just watching the place, see who's coming and going."

"Nate," I said. "What exactly are you doing? This isn't some kind of game, you know."

"I know it's not. But I thought I could help you."

"By sitting outside a restaurant, stalking the bartender?"

"John hung out here a lot, right? Didn't you say that? And like you said, if Brian—"

"Nate, I think you need to get out of there and go home. We can talk tomorrow. Last thing you need is to get yourself in trouble." Alex watched me. I said, "Good night, Nate," and ended the call.

"What was that all about?" Alex said.

I shook my head, not sure I had the right answer. "It sounds like he's on some kind of stakeout."

"Are you kidding?"

I took a deep breath, exhaling as I put the bottle up to my mouth. "I wish I was."

"What was that you said, about Nate stalking someone?"

"Lydia. But I was half kidding. Sort of."

"I'd like to stay here," Alex said. "If it's all right? Besides, you don't have a car. You're going to need the Jeep in the morning, aren't you?"

I nodded. "Are you carrying?"

Alex nodded. "My Glock's downstairs."

"Down below," I said, smiling. "Boat talk."

Alex laughed. "You're not really going to sleep outside, are you?"

I wasn't sure what she was getting at, but I nodded right away. It's comfortable when the weather's a little cooler."

We both stood still for a moment, like neither one knew what to say.

Alex yawned.

"There are blankets down there, if you want to go to sleep now?" I reached onto the boat and grabbed another beer from the cooler. "And you can turn on the AC if it's too warm down there. But it should be cool enough."

124

"Are you sure you're okay out here?" she said. "I feel funny kicking you out of your own bed." She stared back at me for a moment. "You could..." She stopped and turned from me, looking onto the boat. "Can Raz get down there okay?"

"I'll carry him down," I said. "The ladder's tough for a dog."

"So I'll need to lift him up to get him out?"

I shook my head. "I'll get him out when he's ready to come up."

Chapter 18

STRETCHED OUT AND ASLEEP on the cushioned bench on my boat, I fell to the deck when the blanket I had was ripped from my body. Before I could jump to my feet, I had two thick hands wrapped around my neck.

Brian Mason leaned over me with his knee in my chest. His shaved head glowed in the light shining down from the lamp at the corner of the dock.

Choking under his grasp, I grabbed his thick wrists and tried to remove his hands from my throat. But his grip was too strong. I reached up for his bald, sweat-covered head but my hands slipped off.

He took one hand from my throat and tried to throw a punch. But I turned my head and he skimmed my ear, his knuckles hitting the deck beneath me with enough force, he yelped in pain.

It gave me the split second I needed, freeing my neck and driving my knee up into his crotch, throwing him off me.

He stumbled back, and I was up on my feet, throwing two good punches that caught him right in the chin. He caught his footing and came at me, but froze when Raz barked from down below.

"Is that a dog?" he said, although ignoring it. He charged me with his shoulder down. He tackled me like a lineman, slamming into my chest with enough force, it sent me backward.

I tripped over the blanket on the floor and fell on top of the rail at the bow, feeling the crack of my ribs as I landed, barely stopping myself from going overboard.

Brian came at me again and grabbed my shirt, ripping it up and over my head. I wrestled one arm free and threw a wild punch, following it with two more I was sure had connected with his skull.

I pulled my shirt down, and he came at me with a shot that hit me in the nose. I felt the blood in my mouth.

Raz's barking grew louder and more vicious—a side of him I'd never heard—but Alex had remained quiet. I was afraid Brian had already done something to her before waking me up.

"Alex!" I yelled.

Brian wrapped his arms around me and, as if a wrestling move, lifted all two hundred fifteen pounds of me upside down, dropping me on my back. He leaped and drove his knee into my stomach.

Raz came up out of the hole, Alex helping him up the ladder.

Brian let out a scream when Raz clamped his jaws down on his ankle, and it didn't appear he'd let go.

He reached into the waist of his pants and pulled a gun, turning it on Raz. But I was able to reach for one of the aluminum lawn chairs, swinging it at Brian.

The gun fired in the air as I'd knocked him off his feet. That's when Raz dove at Brian's arm and bit into it.

Alex came up out of the hole. "Raz! Heel!" She had her Glock out in front of her, pointed at Brian. "Get up, and move slowly."

Raz moved and sat by her feet.

Brian had dropped his gun but was looking at it, within reach.

"Go for it," Alex said, "And I'll blow a hole right in your chest."

Brian raised his hands up over his head, not saying a word.

I shoved him out of my way and stood next to Alex and Raz, rubbing my sore jaw. "You can shoot him if you'd like," I said. I grinned, and felt blood drip down my chin.

Brian tried to stand, leaning forward with his hands on his knees, trying to catch his breath. "I can't even breathe out my nose because of you. I haven't slept in three days."

"Alex," I said. "I think we should go ahead and call Detective Stone. Tell him we have someone he can fingerprint, that there's a good chance they'll match up with what he pulled from your house."

"Fingerprints? You're really going to call the cops? For this? What kind of a man—"

"It's got little to do with this," I said. "But breaking into Alex's house? Now, that's a different story. And I'd guess you, or someone you know, was behind the wheel of that pickup."

"What are you... I have no idea what you're even..." He looked at Alex. "I didn't break into your house. I've never seen you in my life!"

Alex held the gun on him.

"So, what's the story?" I said. "What are you hiding? And what is killing me going to do to—"

"Who said I was going to kill you? I didn't come here to kill you. I needed to teach you a lesson. You embarrassed me in front of my girlfriend. And in front of my customers."

"*I* embarrassed you?" I laughed. "I'd say you embarrassed yourself."

Brian appeared to be getting agitated. "You're lucky you were saved by some girl and that stupid mutt."

I glanced at Alex. "A *girl*?"

"A girl with a Glock pointed at you," she said, staring down at Brian.

I said, "So, the only thing I can come up with is either you're afraid I'm going to find whatever it is you're hoping I don't, or this is all about you being jealous of Lydia paying me a little too much attention when I was at your bar."

Brain laughed. "Jealous? Of what, an old man?"

I stared back at him and shrugged. "Oh, I don't know if that's as crazy as it sounds. I heard she prefers older men."

Brian jumped up and tried to come at me, but Alex stepped in the way, pointing her gun at his face.

"Back off," she said.

Raz growled.

I said, "Why don't you go ahead and tell me, Brian, why Lydia is so upset about John. Are you sure there wasn't something between them?"

He stared at the muzzle pointed at his face and shook his head. "No way. She would never in a million years..."

"Is that a fact? Or is that what she told you. Because I could see you getting all worked up, getting jealous and crazy like you are right now, watching her flirt at the bar with your father's best friend."

"What are you trying to say? You think I—"

"The way you come after me in your parking lot, and here you are, the middle of the night tracking me down. It seems to me you have a hard time controlling your anger."

Brian showed his empty hands to Alex, keeping them raised, and sat down on the padded bench where I'd been asleep ten minutes before. He said, "I didn't like the idea of you showing up at my restaurant asking questions about my dad's friend. That's all there is to it. John should be allowed to rest in peace."

"That's not up to you to decide," I said.

He stared back at me, shaking his head. "You don't know what you're doing," he said. "Don't you find it strange that Angela's the only one who thinks John's death wasn't an accident? Wouldn't surprise me if she wants to pin something like this on my dad. She'd love to set him up."

"That's ridiculous," I said.

Brian let out a sigh and seemed to have calmed down, although I was about to let my guard down. Without a doubt, the man had a few screws loose. He said, "You got anything to drink?"

I smiled, wondering if maybe the man had two personalities. "You're asking me for a drink after you ripped me out of bed and pounded my face with your first?"

Brian shrugged, grabbing his throat. "I'm thirsty."

"Shouldn't you say please?" I started for the ladder without waiting for his reply. "Keep the gun on him," I said.

Raz kept a low growl.

I came up the ladder with a glass and a bottle of Jack Daniels. I gave Brian a shot.

I picked up the lawn chair I'd whacked Brian with and placed it across from him. I said, "You have to admit, this whole act of yours is making you look very suspicious."

Brian said, "I lost my little brother, you know. He was just a kid. I was young, too. But not too young to see what it did to my family. It was only a matter of time before their marriage fell apart. My mom couldn't take being around here anymore."

"Jacksonville?"

He nodded. "She left me. She left my dad. And she never looked back. Started a whole new life without us."

I glanced back at Alex.

131

She said, "Your mom left you?"

Brian kept his eyes down and didn't answer. "My dad's been through enough. He lost his son. His wife left him. And now, he's lost his best friend. So I'll do whatever I have to do to make sure my dad doesn't get tangled up in whatever it is Angela has planned."

Chapter 19

ALEX AND I STOOD looking up the hill and into the woods at Losco Park, toward the bike trails in the area, where John, according to the sheriff's office, had simply lost control of his bike and flipped it after hitting a tree.

According to the report, John landed at the edge of the lake where he had drowned.

But it didn't seem to make sense. The lake was nearly thirty yards from the trail. "He had to've been riding pretty fast to get off the trail way up there and end up all the way down here."

Alex walked up the grassy hill toward the trail. She slipped at one point, but caught herself before falling to the ground. "It's been a few years since I've been here."

"On a bike?" I said.

She stopped halfway up the hill and turned back to me. "We used to ride, when we were first married."

By "we," Alex was referring to her husband, a fireman, who was tragically killed, rushing into a burning home. The two hadn't even been married a year when she lost him.

I walked along the muddy edge of the lake, then up the hill toward Alex, standing by a group of trees and shrubs in the middle of the grass.

She was gazing at the trees. "Look at this," she said, pointing to one of the taller ones.

I walked over to what she was looking at and saw a fresh chunk missing from the bark. It was at waist height.

"I think this is the tree they believe his handlebar hit," she said.

Alex pointed down the hill, toward a boulder closer to the water, beyond where we stood. "They claim he hit his head on that boulder, losing his helmet in the process."

"That's the part Angela's having trouble with," I said.

"The helmet?"

I nodded, looking at the line from the trail, to the group of trees and shrubs, through to the boulder, then the water. "That's a long way to go, coming off the trail. I would think if he did clip this tree, it would be almost impossible to stay in a straight line. Don't you think?"

Alex didn't respond, her eyes on the report. Although we'd run into plenty of trouble the past two days, I felt it was hard for her to doubt the sheriff's office. She still wasn't comfortable making the connection between whoever it was that had come after us, and what had happened to John on that hill.

"It seems like a lot of speculation here," I said, trudging down toward the water.

"You know how this works," she said. "Whatever we're eventually able to determine, I'm not sure it's going to come from anything at this scene. All anybody can do, whether it's us or the sheriff's office, is to speculate, based on the evidence. And looking at what we have here, it's not out of the realm of possibility that what happened here is anything more than Thompson coming down this hill and losing control."

"Are you saying you're prepared to side with Mason, and anyone else who claims this was a freak accident?"

Alex shook her head. "I'm saying, we're likely not going to have much luck finding much of anything here."

"I'm guessing that's what the investigators said when they showed up. How much time do you really think they put into it?" I nodded toward the report Alex held in her hand. "They made it easy on themselves... couldn't have written up a more generic accident report than the one you're holding." I looked toward the path. "What if he had his bike on the path, and someone knocked him off, dragged him down to the water?"

• • • ● • ● • ● • •

I turned the Jeep's wheels toward the entrance of Michelle Thompson's neighborhood, driving slowly as I approached the gate.

Mickey, the security guard, walked out and seemed to recognize me right away.

"Is this your Jeep?" he said.

I pointed toward Alex with my thumb. "It's hers."

He looked in at Alex and tipped his hat, then glanced back at me, holding his sunglasses slightly off his eyes. "Good. You don't look the type to own a yellow Jeep." He laughed and cleared his throat. "You here to see Mrs. Thompson again? She got home a little while ago."

"We are," I said.

"And I'm guessing she knows you're coming this time?"

"Yes, she's expecting us," I said, although it wasn't true. "You can check with her if you'd like?"

"Nah," Mickey said, walking to the brick guard's station. He reached inside, and the gate slowly slid open. "I'll take your word for it. You seem like an honest man."

· · · · ● · ● ● · ·

Michelle came to the door with something in her mouth, wiping her hands on her white apron hung down past her knees. She finished chewing and invited us inside. "Are you all right?" she said, staring at the bruises on my face.

"This?" I said, pointing to the bruise. "It's nothing. Just a little accident."

"Oh, I'm sorry," she said.

"I know I told you I'd call first before stopping by, but we were in the area and were hoping you'd have some time to continue our conversation?"

Michelle nodded, smiling as she wiped a crumb from the corner of her mouth.

We walked inside to the smell of something sweet and guessed she had again been baking.

I introduced her to Alex. "Michelle, this is my partner, Alex Jepson."

Michelle smiled. "Your partner?"

"We work together," I said.

"Oh, okay, I thought maybe..." She extended her hand. "Michelle Thompson. It's nice to meet you." She waved for us to follow her down the hall. "Please, come into the kitchen. I just pulled a fresh batch of cookies from the oven."

We both followed Michelle down the hall and into the kitchen, but Michelle kept walking. We went outside through the French doors and toward a covered patio, overlooking a small pond and an in-ground pool. The property extended into the golf course behind the house.

Michelle gestured toward a table. "Sit down, let me fix you some tea and cookies." She went back into the house without another word.

Alex had a slight smirk on her face. "Tea and cookies?"

"Betty Crocker," I said. "She was baking cookies last time I was here, too."

Michelle walked out a few moments later with a tray in one hand, and three ice-filled glasses in the other, which she placed on the table. The tray was loaded with cookies. "Here you go," she said. "Let me grab the iced tea."

I waited for her to go back in the house, then whispered to Alex, "She seems like she came out of the nineteen fifties."

Alex didn't respond.

"Even her personality, it's like the bubbly housewives you'd see in the old TV shows, getting things ready before the husband gets home."

Alex cleared her throat as Michelle walked from the house, carrying a glass pitcher to the table.

Michelle filled the three glasses, pushing the plate of cookies toward Alex. "You don't look like you eat a lot of cookies, but I hope you'll try one," she said.

Alex grinned and grabbed a cookie. "Thank you," she said, first taking a sip of tea. "Henry told me you make the best iced tea he's ever had."

Michelle gave Alex a big smile. "I know we're down here in Florida, but I don't like it too sweet. Especially not when I make cookies." She sat down across from me. "So when you say you're partners... how exactly does that work?"

"How does it *work*?" Alex said, like she wasn't sure what she meant. "I run the security staff for the Sharks. And in the off-season, I help Henry when he needs it."

"The Sharks? Is that the baseball team?"

Alex nodded.

"That's interesting," Michelle said. "Although I imagine being a PI is a lot of excitement. More than being a security guard?" She smiled, but looked like she wasn't sure if she should.

Alex took a bite from her cookie.

Michelle held her glass, leaning with her arms resting on the table. "I know you're here to talk about John. But, the truth is, I've been doing all I can since the accident to *not* think about him." She reached for the tray of cookies, grabbed one and took a bite. "That's why I've been baking so much lately. Just to keep myself busy."

Alex reached for Michelle's hand. "I know it must be hard for you."

"Well, the way my mom used to say it was when life knocks you down, you have to wipe the dirt off your knees and get right back up."

I reached for a cookie, broke off a piece and popped it in my mouth. "I know you'd rather have a different conversation, but if, for now, can you tell us about your relationship with John? Was everything okay between you?"

Michelle didn't look like she liked the question. "I'm sorry, why would you ask about my relationship with John?"

I didn't want to make any of this harder on Michelle than it already was. But I needed some answers. "To be honest," I said, "I want to establish what your marriage was like, in case, well...

in case there could have potentially been something else going on with him. I mean, outside of your marriage."

Michelle let out a sigh, nodding. "Like any good marriage, we still had our ups and downs." She seemed to force a smile. "Everything's not always tea and cookies."

Alex and I sat quiet, watching to see where she was going.

She continued, "John spent a lot of time working. That was his real love. His business. His work. Of course, he had his friends, too. And business associates..."

Alex said, "Did he spend a lot of time here, at home over the past few months?"

Michelle said, "I guess he was home as much as any other hardworking man. He traveled a bit, but mostly regionally. Sometimes he'd stay overnight so he didn't have to drive home late. Of course, John would never drink and drive, so he'd call me if he had too much to drink while out with clients. He'd get a hotel room."

"Oh," I said. "I guess that's good, right?" I sipped my tea and gave Alex a quick glance before I said to Michelle, "When was the last time John went away?"

Michelle topped off each of our glasses with more iced tea. "Actually, he was out of town the days leading up to..." She stayed quiet for a handful of seconds. "The last time I saw him, other than when he was asleep in our bed, was the Thursday before he left."

I said, "Thursday? He was on the road until..." I thought for a moment. "When did he get back?"

"He went up to Georgia to meet with a new client. He didn't come home until Saturday evening. He told me they went out to dinner Friday night, and he golfed with them Saturday."

"But didn't you see him when he got home? Or Sunday morning, before he went out on his bike?"

Michelle hesitated a moment, then let out a choking cough. She grabbed a napkin and covered her mouth, then reached for her glass of tea, taking a sip. She swallowed and slapped herself on the chest.

Alex and I both jumped from our seats, like one of us was going to have to perform the Heimlich maneuver. "Are you all right?" I said.

But Michelle held up her hand, shaking us both off. She coughed for another few seconds and cleared her throat. "Oh my. I'm sorry. I was choking on a cookie." She took another sip of tea and placed the glass on the table. "What was your question?"

"I was wondering when you saw him last," I said, sitting back in my seat.

Michelle took another drink, once again clearing her throat. "I was out when John got home Saturday night. I had gone out for a drink at the club."

Alex said, "What's the 'club'?"

"Deerwood. The country club."

"The one right here, in your neighborhood?" I said.

"Yes, but you still have to drive a couple of miles to get to the entrance."

I said, "You must've spoken to him on the phone, once he got home?"

She shook her head. "He was in bed early. And John hated to be woken up once he was asleep. I knew he'd be tired, so I didn't bother him." She stared at me without a word, for a moment. "I had a few drinks. If I'd known I would have never..." She closed her eyes, and a tear came down her cheek. "I went to bed, trying to be very quiet. And when I woke up in the morning, John was already gone."

Chapter 20

ANGELA RAISED HER GLASS, watching me walk up the step to where she was seated on the far side of the bar at Barrington's restaurant.

Her eyes widened as I walked closer. "What happened to your face?"

I touched one of the many bruises. "Brian Mason stopped by my boat for a drink."

I sat down on the padded leather stool next to her, and the bartender, Kyle, came right over. "Whoa, what happened?"

I didn't think it was that bad, but I guess it was.

"Nothing a glass of Jack can't fix," I said.

He turned with a nod and walked away.

Angela was still staring at me, like she'd never seen a man with a banged-up face. "Did Brian really do that to you?" Her eyes went to my hands, likely noticing my cracked, red knuckles. She said, "Is this the part where you say, 'you should see the other guy'?"

I cracked a smile, watching Kyle as I waited for my drink.

"He's one of the best bartenders in the city, you know. And he's quite the looker, isn't he?"

I said to Angela, "A *looker*?"

She said, "You can appreciate another man's good looks, can't you?" Angela looked around the bar. "See all these women? They're all here because of Kyle."

But I'd noticed just as many men, in their fancy suits and ties, as females.

Do you know why all these men are here?" She nodded toward Kyle. "It all starts with him. The women come in, and the men follow. That's why I've always said attractive employees are good for business."

Kyle put the glass of Jack down in front of me.

"What about John?" I said. "Did he hang around here?"

"He used to," she said. "John was no different than these other men, like a hound tracking a scent. He'd come here, usually looking for someone to fool around with. I'm sure it worked out for him once or twice. But once I started hanging around, he stopped coming."

"You don't mean while you were married, do you?"

Angela shook her head. "No. John was actually somewhat discreet when we were married. But barely."

"He wasn't faithful?"

She laughed. "I hope you ask better questions of your suspects."

"Keep in mind," I said, "we haven't really discussed much about your personal life, or your marriage with John. It was a simple question, and thought maybe you could answer without—"

"I'm playing with you, Henry. Do you always take things so seriously?" She turned in her seat, toward me. "Of *course*, John cheated on me. A man with three different wives is usually going to have a hard time being faithful, don't you think?" She lifted her glass and held it in front of her lips. "He slept with his second wife while we were still married. Not that I didn't see it coming."

I said, "Do you want to tell me what happened?"

"Do you really need me to rehash *that* old story?"

"You don't have to, but you never know what kind of significance it could have on the case."

Angela sipped her drink and placed the glass on the bar. "We were at a conference out in Tennessee, an event put on by the International Insurers Association. We'd go every year, where a whole bunch of us from the industry would get together. We all knew each other over the years, so it would be like a big family reunion. Once in a while someone would drop out of the business or stop coming for whatever reason. Otherwise, it was pretty much the same crowd, and we'd party for three nights straight, then go back to reality until the next year."

"Theresa was part of this group?" I said.

Angela nodded. "It's funny, but at the time I actually considered her a good friend. But she was always flirting with the

145

men, especially John. She made it seem like she was joking around, having fun. But I always knew she had something for him." She pulled out her red lipstick and ran it over her lips. "She had Nate at the time, too."

"At the conference?"

Angela laughed. "No, what I mean is she was a single mom. He must've been nine or ten at the time. But we all used to joke behind her back, that she was looking for a daddy for Nate. Problem was, the men she flirted with were usually married."

I finished my drink and slid the glass across the bar. "So, did John and Theresa—"

"Listen for a moment, and I'll tell you the whole story." She shifted in her seat. "One night, I ended up feeling sick. Not from too many drinks, either. I was actually sick. I thought maybe it was the flu, but it didn't matter. I wanted to get out of there. The last place I wanted to be was in a hotel room with a fever of one hundred and two."

"Did you leave?"

"I tried to. Airline couldn't get me out of there until the next day. Only thing I could do was go to the airport, on standby, hoping I'd get on a flight." She grinned, her lips tight. "John was pushing me to go home to be comfortable and get better. But he wasn't about to leave with me." She let out a slight laugh. "I should've realized what he was up to."

I said, "He didn't even think about leaving?"

"John?" She laughed, shifting in her seat as she turned, facing the bar, the stem of her martini glass between her fingers.

"Turns out, I couldn't even get a flight on standby. There was no way I was getting out of there, so my only option was to take a cab back to the hotel."

I started to see where Angela might've been heading with the story.

"John, of course, was staying in the room. So I never bothered to check out, and never turned in my room key." She paused, looking straight ahead across the bar, like she wasn't sure she wanted to finish. "I slid the card in the door and pushed it open, and there's John, with his ass sticking up in the air. Theresa and those pretty blue eyes looked out from under him, staring at me in the doorway, my suitcase in my hand."

Angela tried to smile, acting like it no longer bothered her. But I could tell it did. It was a long time ago, but telling me what happened seemed to reopen her wounds.

"Kyle," she said, her voice quiet. She lifted her empty glass to him, and he gave a nod.

Angela cleared her throat. "There's *business*. And there's *pleasure*. You try to keep them separate, but it's not as easy as it sounds." Kyle brought her another martini and placed it on the bar. She said, "We work most of our waking hours, for most of our lives. Like dogs, sometimes. For most people, that's what life is all about: our work. It's one life. This work-life-balance crap you hear, give me a break."

"I don't know how you kept the business going," I said.

"Well, we almost didn't. In the early days, when we were still young, we did our best to keep our personal lives separate from the business. Somehow, we managed to make it all work. But after that night, I had no choice but to get over what he did. If I hadn't, the business—like our marriage—would have never survived."

"And here you are," I said, "the only person in John's life who refused to believe what everyone else is saying."

Angela ran her finger around the stem of her glass. "I believe most people would rather hide from the truth than try to face it."

My glass was somehow empty again, except for the two pieces of ice at the bottom. "So, should I assume John also cheated on Michelle?"

"I'd be more surprised if he hadn't."

"But you don't know," I said.

She shook her head. "No. And I don't think I care."

"Not even if it had something to do with what happened to him?"

She lifted her glass. "If he did cheat on her, of course it would've been with someone much younger. I wouldn't be surprised if John had already been wondering if Michelle was already too old for him."

I started to laugh but realized she wasn't making a joke.

"Michelle's thirty-seven," she said. "If I had to guess, John's fling would be with some hot young woman in her twenties."

"Yeah?"

Angela shrugged. "John could be charming enough when he wanted to be." She sipped her drink. "And he was never shy about telling people how much money he had, either, which for some women is like a magnet."

We both sat quiet, and I thought back to my conversation with Michelle. "Do you know where John was the Thursday night before that Sunday? Michelle told me he was out of town, meeting with a client?"

Angela appeared somewhat perplexed. "Michelle said that?"

"She said that was the last time she saw him, face-to-face. Except when he was sleeping."

Angela was quiet, her eyes a bit narrowed, like she was trying to think it through. "She didn't say which client, did she?"

"No. That's why I'm asking. I was hoping you might know. The only thing she said was that he was in Georgia, and he didn't come back until Saturday."

"Georgia?" Angela shook her head, an expression on her face like she was still thinking. "We don't have clients in Georgia. And why would he stay through Saturday?"

"Michelle said he played golf."

Angela didn't seem to have an answer. "I didn't always know where he was. He could've been out, looking for business. He wouldn't always tell me, and I learned over the years not to ask."

"If it was business," I said, "there must be records, right? Receipts? The hotel invoice?"

Angela took a moment, then nodded. "You could ask Kayla. I know, over the past year, she'd go out with him to meet potential customers. I heard him make a joke once, maybe around Roy, and said if it was a male client, he could get a signed contract any time Kayla was present in the room."

Chapter 21

I FOLLOWED KAYLA MORTON down the hall at Thompson Insurance, toward her office. I stopped at a large corner office with the door open but the lights off. There was a leather couch and a small round table, with interesting framed art hung on the walls. Even with the lights off, the office was bright from the sun shining through the windows. Like Angela's office, it overlooked the St. Johns River.

Kayla stopped past the doorway. "That's John's office. Nobody's even walked in there since..." She stepped to the doorway, taking her time, staring at the empty desk facing out. She turned and again continued down the hall.

I followed. "Nobody's been in his office? Does that include the sheriff?"

She glanced back at me and nodded before walking into another office, much smaller and less inviting than Angela's or John's. It was closer to the size of a walk-in closet, with a desk and even a small blue couch that barely fit, to the side of the door. Kayla went and sat behind her desk, with two chairs across from her. "Please, have a seat."

The seat I sat in was uncomfortable, with the padding worn and flattened under the faux leather, the hard wood underneath pressing into me. I shifted, wondering if I should move to the couch.

The only window was on the wall behind Kayla, with a view, not of the river, but the parking lot.

Kayla stood. "I'm sorry, I didn't even ask if you'd like a drink. What would you like, a coffee?"

"That's okay," I said. "You don't have to..."

"No, please. Let me get you something. I insist."

I watched her walk to the door.

"Coffee is fine," I said. "But—"

"How do you like it?"

"Black is good."

She walked away without another word, and I turned around looking at the framed pictures hanging on the wall. One was a piece of art that looked like a child had drawn it, although I wasn't sure it was meant to. There was another larger framed photo, with two children posing in front of a plain, gray background, like it'd been taken at Sears.

Kayla had never been married. At least as far as I knew.

I turned the only frame on her desk to look at it. The photo was of a white-haired man and a woman who looked younger and a lot like Kayla.

"My parents," Kayla said, walking through the door behind me.

"Oh, I'm sorry. I was..."

She put a steaming mug, with the Thompson Insurance logo on it, down on the desk. "Isn't that part of your job? To snoop around?" She smiled, but it seemed forced.

Kayla sat on the small couch behind me, and I turned my chair to face her. She straightened her skirt, crossing her long legs. She was quiet, staring at me like she was waiting for me to say something else.

I looked at the photo of the two kids. "They're not yours, are they?"

She laughed. "I would've had to have had them in my teens." She stared at the photo. "That's my niece and nephew."

"I assumed you were too young to have kids that age," I said. "But, I guess you never know." I turned and grabbed my mug from the desk. There was a somewhat awkward feeling in the room. "How old are you, if you don't mind me asking?"

"I just turned twenty-nine."

I did the math. "So you were twenty-two when you started working here? For John?"

She nodded. "I was actually twenty-three, if you don't include the unpaid internship, when I worked alongside the office manager." She shook her head. "She was a horrible person. I was going to quit, I hated her so much. But then John asked me if I was good with computers. When I told him I was, he hired me to be his assistant."

I sipped my coffee. "So you've known John a decent amount of time. Longer than his own wife?"

She nodded, twisting a strand of hair around her finger. "He made me a VP a year later."

"VP?"

"Vice president."

"I know what it means. That's quite a jump to go from being an unpaid intern to vice president in such a short amount of time, isn't it?"

She nodded. "He had just fired his VP of account services, so the position was open."

I took another sip of coffee and placed the mug on the desk. "It sounds like you were around when he married Theresa?"

She adjusted her skirt. "I was. I remember the first time I met her, at a surprise birthday party she threw for John at her house. I'd only been working for him for a short time, and I remember hearing about it, but wasn't even sure why I'd be invited."

"I assume you were?"

Kayla nodded. "Theresa planned the whole thing by herself, really going out of her way to make it a big deal. I remember being there, feeling out of place, like I didn't belong. She hadn't invited everyone from the office. I realized later she only invited me because she needed my help making sure he didn't find out about it."

"Was Angela there?"

Kayla shook her head. "That would've been weird."

"What about Michelle?"

Kayla seemed to roll her eyes. "Michelle was Nate's nanny. Actually, I don't know if she was still technically the nanny by that point, but she worked for her. More like her gofer. Theresa's slave."

"Her *slave*?"

"Theresa had her running around all day, serving food and drinks to the guests. I almost felt bad for her, the way Theresa treated her. Michelle didn't seem to be having a very good time."

Kayla held her gaze on me, like she wanted a response.

"What about you and Theresa, did you get along?"

"I guess so. But Theresa was a jealous woman. She was jealous of any other female John would talk to. He told me she'd asked about me, more than once."

"Oh yeah?"

Kayla shifted in her seat, like she couldn't get comfortable. "I'm sorry, but what does this all have to do with? You know Theresa's dead, right?"

I nodded. "I'm trying to get my brain wrapped around all of John's relationships. He had some interesting ones."

Kayla said, "John was a good man."

"Was there ever more between you and John? I mean, besides him being your boss?"

Kayla frowned, shaking her head. "What? No! *Never!* I don't think I like where you're going with these questions."

"I told you, I'm trying to..."

155

She stood from the couch, crossing her arms. "You shouldn't assume because I cared about John as a person that there was ever anything between us."

I stood from the chair. "Can you tell me about the trip to Georgia?"

Kayla swallowed hard, staring back at me without responding.

"Listen," I said. "I'm not trying to imply you're guilty of anything just because you may have gone on a work trip with John. But I'd like to know the truth. Were you there with him?"

She cleared her throat, twisting her hair around her finger. "I know a lot about the insurance business. John used to say I knew more than most people who'd been in this business for thirty years."

"Are you trying to say you were there?"

She walked past me, around her desk, and to the window. With her back to me, she stayed quiet, rubbing her hands up and down her arms like she was trying to break a chill.

She didn't have to tell me she'd gone with him. Her actions made it clear.

I said, "Did you stay with him?"

Kayla took a moment, finally shaking her head. "No, I didn't stay with him."

"But you did stay Friday night?"

Kayla sat at her desk, doing her best to avoid looking me in the eye. "I came home Friday, right after the meeting. I have no idea what John did after that. But I came home, and went to bed." She raised her gaze to mine. "Alone."

Chapter 22

I'D PICKED UP ALEX after leaving Thompson Insurance and stopped by the sheriff's office, where a friend of Alex's was able to get her a copy of the report from the night Theresa Thompson was found dead in her home. We hadn't had a chance to review it but were on our way out to talk to Nate.

My phone rang, and it was Kayla. "I wonder what she wants," I said. After the way my meeting had gone with her, I didn't think I'd hear from her so soon after leaving.

"Henry, listen. After you left, I was able to get my hands on a copy of Theresa's life insurance policy. The one Nate wants."

I said, "I thought you said it wasn't a policy held by Thompson Insurance?"

"It's not," she said. "I called Eric. He knew where it was."

"John's brother?"

"Yes. He has a contact, and was able to get it for me."

I glanced at the clock on the dash. "Can I swing by your office right now? I'm only about ten minutes away."

"No, not right now. I'd rather... I don't want Angela to know what I'm doing. In fact, I think it's best she doesn't know anything about it. Not right now."

"Why?" I said. "She's my client. I'm not sure I can—"

"Henry, please. I'm sorry. I'm asking you to do me this favor." The line went quiet. "Can you come by my apartment this evening? I'll bring the policy home and can make a copy for you."

I wasn't sure why Kayla wanted to keep it quiet. It wouldn't make sense that Angela would care, one way or the other. I assumed it would have little to do with her, and considering the policy could potentially help Nate get something he could be owed, I believed she'd be all for it. But Kayla didn't sound like she was going to budge. "Okay," I said.

"I could give it to Nate," she said. "But I thought it made more sense, since, well, who knows. Maybe it could tie into what happened to John?"

"I can't answer that," I said.

She was quiet again with a long pause on the other end. "I know how you think it looks... about me and John. So, I guess I'm hoping that since I'm helping you with this, maybe you can keep things quiet?"

"I'm sorry, Kayla. But I'm not exactly clear on what you're trying to say. You told me there was nothing between you and John, so—"

"Come to my apartment at seven, okay? I can explain a little more." She hung up without another word.

I said to Alex, "Kayla Morton has a copy of Theresa Thompson's life insurance policy." I looked ahead, toward the road, thinking.

"What's wrong?" Alex said.

I wasn't sure. I said, "There's something about her. Kayla. I just can't put my finger on it. She said she'd explain more when I got over there tonight."

"More about what?"

I shrugged, shaking my head. "I don't know. I guess we'll find out."

Alex shifted in her seat, looking straight ahead. "I won't be able to go with you," she said. "I hope that's okay?"

"Why not?"

She paused, and I could tell there was something she didn't want to tell me. "I have plans."

"Oh, okay."

We were both quiet for a few moments.

I said, "Is it a date?"

She laughed. "None of your business." But after a couple of moments, she said, "I'm meeting someone."

"You can't tell me who?"

She held the manilla folder in her hand. "Chris, from the sheriff's office. He's the one who got me this report."

My first thought, aside from the fact I'd never met her friend, was that I didn't have any wheels of my own. "Are you going to need your Jeep?"

I could tell by the look on her face the answer was yes. "I thought Billy said he had a car for you?"

"He does. But I haven't had a chance to go pick it up." I smiled. "But I'm enjoying the Jeep. Even if it *is* yellow."

• • • ● • ● • • •

Alex and I turned into the parking lot at a place called Rewind Records, where Nate had been working part-time.

The small, one-level building looked old with white paint peeling from the brick exterior. The windows were covered in posters of album covers and famous musicians like Tom Petty and Johnny Cash. There was a poster of Billy Idol, from when he was younger, with his white spiked hair and snarled lip.

Alex had been quiet for most of the ride, her eyes on the medical examiner's report on her lap. She said, "Theresa had a blood alcohol level of point one three eight when she died."

"That's a lot of booze," I said.

Alex continued, "She had a cracked skull, a fractured hip, and a broken neck, excessive blood loss due to her fall, and a puncture wound from a broken wineglass found underneath her at the scene."

"She held on to it all the way down the stairs?"

"Held on to *what*?"

"The wineglass. You fall down the stairs... most people would drop the glass and at least try to grab the railing?"

161

I picked up the folder between us and opened it up to the original police report Alex had gotten from her friend. I skimmed over the handwritten report. "She was home alone, and Nate was at his aunt's house. Theresa had traveled out of town, but came back a day earlier than expected." I looked over at Alex. "This is all according to John, who arrived home at two in the morning and found her at the bottom of the stairs." I ran my finger along the words in the report. "He was allegedly at a friend's house, playing cards."

Alex said, "Does it say who the friend is?"

"Roy Mason." I said.

Alex stared back at me. "He was at Roy's house, playing cards when his wife died?"

"John claimed he had no idea she'd gotten home a day earlier than expected. It says here he thought maybe she wanted to surprise him."

Alex had a twisted look on her face. "Surprise him? Didn't he talk to her at some point? Wouldn't she call him to—"

"I'm just telling you what's here." I looked toward the Rewind Records sign on the building. "Looks like I'll have to talk to Roy again, see how much he remembers about his poker game."

I put the report back in the folder. "Let me go see if Nate's available." I stepped down from the Jeep and walked up to the entrance. It didn't seem to be a very busy place, considering nobody had gone in or come out while we sat in the parking lot. But I didn't think much of it until I pulled on the door's handle. It was locked.

I leaned into the glass and tried to see through what little space there was between the posters and signs taped on the glass.

Alex stuck her head out from the Jeep. "Are they closed?"

I turned but didn't answer, trying to find another way to see inside. I put my face close to the window, near the Billy Idol poster, and had a better view inside.

I saw a pair of sneakers on the floor, and realized they were on someone's feet. That someone was lying on the floor. Conscious or not, I had no idea. All I could see, sticking out from an aisle, were black Converse high-top sneakers.

I stepped to the door and pounded on the glass. I yelled for Alex, "Your gun! Give me your gun!"

Alex jumped from the Jeep and rushed toward me, holding out her Glock. "What are you doing? What's wrong?"

"There's someone on the floor inside."

I shook the door's handle as if I could rip it from the frame. "Step back," I said, putting my arm out to keep Alex away from the door.

I pointed the gun low on the plate glass and pulled the trigger. The glass shattered, falling almost completely from the metal frame. I reached my hand through the opening and turned the lock inside, opening the door. As soon as I saw the body, I said, "Call nine-one-one."

I ran in and crouched next to what appeared to be a young man, bleeding.

His eyes were open, and he grabbed my arm. "Help... Help me. Somebody shot me."

"Stay down," I said, trying to see where he'd been hit. It looked like the bullet got him just under his shoulder. "You'll be okay," I said. "EMTs are on their way."

He tried to sit up. "Don't move," I said, looking around at the place. "Do you work here?"

He nodded.

"Were you robbed?"

"I don't know. I don't think so."

"Where's Nate?" I said. "I thought he was working?"

The young man turned his head toward another door at the back of the building with a red Emergency Exit sign over it. "He ran out the back way. I... I don't know if he got away from whoever did this or not."

Alex was standing over us.

"Stay with him," I said.

I got up on my feet and ran out the back door.

Chapter 23

WE WALKED OUT OF the sheriff's office and turned down East Bay, toward Alex's Jeep. Alex said, "You heard what they said. Without any evidence something actually happened to Nate, there's a good chance he's out there somewhere on the run."

Her Jeep was within view, parked at the end of the block. "I wish I'd gone in that store sooner," I said.

"I know that young man said it'd only happened a few minutes before we got in there. But we would've heard the gunshot. So, I'm not sure you should feel like there was something you could've done, because I'm not sure there was."

I pulled the keys from my pocket, and Alex took them from my hand. "I'm going to drive," she said.

"I guess that means I need to get to Billy's and pick up that car? Do you have time to drive me out there?"

She stepped up into the driver's seat. "I'm supposed to meet Chris at seven thirty. And if you're still going to Kayla's apartment..."

"I'm not walking," I said. "If that's what you're about to say?"

Alex turned the key in the ignition. "You can take the Jeep. Just drop me off on your way out to Kayla's."

"I'm supposed to be there at seven," I said. "Where are you meeting your friend?"

Alex pulled out of the parking space, continued on East Bay, and turned onto North Liberty. "I have to confirm, but maybe I can meet him at Billy's Place."

"That works, as long as you don't mind. I can drop you off, come back to get you unless... I wouldn't want to interrupt your date."

Alex kept her eyes on the road, ignoring me as she turned onto 115. "You know it's not a date," she said. "So you can just knock it off."

I looked toward the Mathews Bridge, off in the distance. "Why are you going *this* way?"

"I need to go home and change."

"What's wrong with what you're wearing? If it's not a date, then—"

"Am I really supposed to go out dressed like this?" She gave me another one of her looks. "Why are you acting like this?"

We crossed over the St. Johns, and I knew I was acting like an idiot, with remarks I didn't need to make that gave her the impression I might've been a little jealous. Maybe I was. "How come you never mentioned this guy Chris's name before?"

"I didn't know he'd gotten a job with the sheriff's office. I already told you, we were in the academy together. But we'd lost touch."

"I don't remember you saying anything about it."

"Well, there's not much to tell," she said.

We were both quiet, and I could see her smiling, her eyes on the road ahead.

"What's so funny?" I said.

She glanced at me, the smile still there. "I was thinking of how Chris and I had become friends. He got into some trouble in the academy, and I stuck my neck out for him."

"So he's a good guy?" I said.

Alex nodded. "He helped us out, didn't he?"

I was quiet, looking toward the water. "Does he get along with Stone?"

She shrugged. "I think so, although they've banged heads a couple of times."

"Well then, maybe Chris is all right."

She shifted lanes. "But I wish you wouldn't be so hard on Mike. He rubs a lot of people the wrong way, but once they get to know him..."

I said, "I've gotten to know him. And he still rubs me the wrong way."

We drove another couple of miles and turned down Alex's road. I reached into the glove box and pulled out her Glock.

She pulled in her driveway, then spied her gun. "Maybe you should hold on to that? I have another one inside." She stepped out and walked onto the porch, opening the front door.

I hurried up inside after her, and practically shoved her aside so I could look around, seeing that I was the one holding the gun.

But Alex grabbed my arm. "I don't think there's anything to worry about." She walked into the kitchen and turned on the light. "It's quiet when Raz isn't here." She smiled. "I think he likes staying at Billy's."

"He likes the food," I said.

Alex turned on the light in the hall. "But I feel better that he's not here by himself." She walked into the room on the right and went to the closet where she stored her guns. She unlocked the door, unlocked the safe, and came out with another handgun. "I'm going up to take a shower," she said. "Help yourself to a beer."

I didn't hesitate to grab a drink, taking a beer from the refrigerator. I checked my phone to see if Nate had called me back after the dozen or so times I'd called him. Each call gave me the same generic message, indicating his voicemail hadn't been set up.

I went outside on the porch and called Billy, told him what'd happened to Nate and about the kid who was shot in the store.

Billy said, "And the sheriff's office still won't believe you that any of this has something to do with John Thompson?"

"They're not saying much at all right now. One of the officers on the scene said the area has a lot of crime, and it's not out of the ordinary for places to get robbed."

"Did they take anything?" Billy said.

"Not a thing. But the same officer said Alex and I could have scared him off when we pulled into the parking lot."

"Nobody knows where Nate is? Do you know where he lives?"

"Nate was sleeping on the kid's couch, the one who was shot."

"What about family?" Billy said. "Doesn't he have anyone living in the area?"

I sat in the rocking chair and sipped my beer. "Only relative I'm aware of is the aunt he used to live with. But she's down in Gainesville. I'm going to see if I can find her number."

Billy was quiet.

"You there?" I said.

"Yeah, I'm here. But I gotta run. Keep me updated."

"Will do," I said, about to hang up.

Billy said, "Wait!"

"Yeah?"

"Did you go by my house yet? Pick up the car?"

"Not yet," I said. "We were planning to, until all this happened. Alex said she'll drive me over there to get it in the morning."

169

"I know you're not excited about it, but it's not a bad car, you know. Needs some work, but it runs all right. I have a feeling you'll like it."

"Hey, how's Raz?" I said. "Alex will want to know."

"Raz is good, although it seems like he's wondering why he's here, and not at his house. He keeps climbing on the couch, looking out the window."

"Well, it's a nice view," I said.

"Chloe took him for a walk, but she said the same thing. It's like something's bothering him."

"Don't forget, he was pretty much abandoned before Alex got him. I'm sure it's on his mind."

"Okay, well, tell her he's fine," Billy said.

"Alex will be there soon," I said. "I'm dropping her off. She's meeting a friend."

"Here?" he said. "Who's the friend?"

"A deputy with the sheriff's office. I'm sure you'll get to meet him."

Chapter 24

By the time I got to Kayla's apartment, it was close to eight o'clock. Eight forty-seven, to be exact. I was late, stepping out from the Jeep. I checked my phone to make sure I hadn't missed a call.

I looked up along the front of the building at the balconies running up the side of it and knew one of them was Kayla's, but I didn't know which one.

It was dark outside, and about half of the apartments appeared dark inside. Others were well-lit, looking from where I stood. Voices came from somewhere up above and sounded like tenants having a good time, maybe hanging out on their balconies. But I didn't see anyone.

I walked under a covered area toward the lobby and tried to open the glass door. The door was locked, and there didn't appear to be anyone coming in or going out. So I pressed the button for Kayla's apartment. There was no sound or buzz when I pushed the button, so I could only assume it worked. I thought maybe someone would show up in the lobby and let me in.

I waited, but there was no response from Kayla. The doors didn't buzz, as I'd hoped.

I waited at least a half minute, maybe a little less, then pressed the button again. I'd already been to her apartment and knew I had the right number, but checked the paper in my pocket anyway, just in case.

I had the right place. But after pushing the button a third time, there was still no response.

I pulled out my phone and dialed her number, the call ringing six times before her voicemail came on:

This is Kayla, you know what to do at the beep.

The phone beeped. "Hey, Kayla? It's Henry. I know I'm a little late—sorry about that—but I'm downstairs now, standing outside the lobby. I think I have the right apartment: number seven-two-oh—"

There was a loud thump that came from somewhere behind me, followed by bloodcurdling screams. The laughter I'd heard coming from the balconies was gone. I ran from the building's entrance and around the corner.

In front of me, a few feet away on the sidewalk, was a motionless body.

I looked upward, where people were looking over the edges of their balconies, screaming and crying.

I yelled, "Somebody call nine-one-one!" then ran over to what was clearly a woman's body. She was facedown. But as soon as I stepped closer, I recognized the hair.

I turned her over and saw her face, eyes open, as if she were looking right at me.

But there was nothing in her blank stare. I checked her pulse but knew there wouldn't be one.

Kayla Morton was dead.

• • • • ● • ● • • • •

Detective Mike Stone took a drag of his cigarette and looked at the crowd in front of Kayla's building. "Why can't you answer a simple question? Do you really expect me to believe you just happen to've been here when a woman jumped from her balcony?"

I leaned against the front of the Jeep with my arms crossed, looking at the ground. "I don't know what to tell you."

"You don't, huh?" Mike took a step closer. "If you don't tell me why you were here, I'm going to get one of those officers over there to throw you in the back of a car and lock you up for the night. Then we'll see how much talking you'll do."

I stared back at Mike and knew he wasn't about to let it slide. "I know her because she works for Angela Thompson."

Mike was about to take a drag from his cigarette but stopped. "You're not going to try and tell me this has something to do with John Thompson's—"

"Why are you so thickheaded?" I said, straightening up from the Jeep. "I don't understand why you and your friends at that sheriff's office have refused to make the connection. I swear, if I didn't know any better, I'd think someone over there was on the take."

Through gritted teeth, Mike said, "Watch yourself, Walsh."

"I'm just saying," I said. "I don't get why I'm the only one who—"

"You seem to have all the answers, but you still haven't told me exactly what you were doing here."

I was hesitant to tell him too much. But I wasn't sure I had a choice. "She was supposed to give me something. But I never made it up to her apartment. I was over there, outside the lobby."

Mike said, "So she was expecting you?"

I nodded. "Yeah, but I was supposed to be here at seven. It was a little before eight when I showed up."

Mike gazed toward Kayla Morton's body, covered on the sidewalk where she fell. "Witnesses say you were screaming for someone to let you in."

"She was already dead. I thought I could get up there, maybe find someone up there. Or at least see someone trying to slip out."

Mike stared at me, holding his gaze. "There's no sign of a forced entry."

"So it's someone she knows," I said. I thought about the white truck.

"There's no indication there was anyone else in that apartment."

"What are you saying?" I said.

Mike started to walk away but stopped. "Did it ever cross your mind, Miss Morton may have jumped from that balcony herself?"

• • • • • • • • • •

Angela opened the door wearing gym shorts and a slinky top, exposing most of her stomach. She had a glass of wine in one hand and a bunched-up ball of tissues in the other. She'd been crying.

She looked me in the eye, shaking her head. "I can't believe it, Henry. I can't." She waved for me to come inside.

As soon as I crossed the threshold, she threw her arms around me and cried, her wet face against my chest. But then I felt something drip down my back. It was her wine.

"Oh no," she said, realizing what had happened. She let go and backed away, turning me around so she could look. "I'm so sorry. Can I see if there's something else you can put on?" She sniffled, wiping her nose. "I have some shirts in the closet that may fit you."

"It's fine," I said.

Angela walked into the main living area and sat on the couch. "Are they sure it was suicide?"

Mike had indicated it was a possibility, but I wasn't sure where Angela would have heard it. "I'm not sure at all that's what happened."

"That's what they're saying," she said. "It was on the news."

I shook my head, even though I was starting to wonder. "I don't think so. And the truth is it's too early. The sheriff's office was still investigating when I left. I'd say the news media's speculating right now."

Angela closed her eyes and started to cry again. She dabbed her eyes with the balled-up tissue, sipping her wine. She stared up at me. "You haven't told me what you were doing there tonight. Is there something I should know?"

I thought about not telling her the whole story, but it was only because Kayla had asked me not to. At that point, it didn't make much of a difference. "She'd gotten me some information. For a friend, actually."

"A friend?" She stared at me, waiting for more.

"It was Theresa's life insurance policy."

Angela cocked her head back. "Theresa? John's Theresa?" She was shocked. "Why are you—"

"It was for Nate," I said. "He wants to know why his mother didn't leave him any money when she died. He believes John kept his share."

"But why would Kayla have that policy? We don't offer life insurance, and even if we did—"

"She found the agency that held the policy. In fact, she said Eric even helped her."

"Eric?" Angela shook her head, covering her eyes with her hand. "I don't understand," she said. "Why was something like this going on behind my back? Aren't I your client? And how did you... When did Nate... How did you find him?"

"He found me," I said. "But, now he's missing."

"He's missing? In what way?"

I looked over at the bar and thought about getting a drink.

"Oh, I'm so sorry," Angela said, as if she'd read my mind. "I'm not thinking clearly. Would you like me to fix you something? I have plenty of Jack, but—"

"I don't think so," I said. "Not now."

"Not even a beer?"

I shook my head. "Thanks, but..."

She walked past me and sat on one of the stools at the bar. "Where is Nate now? I haven't seen him in—"

"He's missing," I said. "Did you hear about the shooting, at a place called Rewind Records? I assume it was on the news, but—"

"I turned it off, once I heard Kayla's name."

"Well, he could be hiding," I said. "He was working at the store, where the shooting took place. The manager who was shot said Nate ran out the back door."

Angela said, "But, who asked Kayla to get the life insurance policy? You? Or Nate?"

"Well, Nate. But I asked her about it, and when she found a way to get a copy of it, she called me. I went to her apartment to pick it up."

Angela finished her wine. "So what's the story with the life insurance policy?"

I held my gaze on Angela. "You really don't know?"

She paused, then finally shook her head. "Know *what*?"

"That John was the sole beneficiary of that policy when Theresa died?"

"Why *would* I know that? It was none of my business."

"I thought you'd know that, after Theresa died, John was suddenly two million dollars richer."

Chapter 25

IT WAS ALREADY PAST midnight when I walked into Billy's Place. It was mostly quiet, other than one of the late-night shows playing on the TV.

Billy was hanging steaming glasses from the dishwasher, sliding them up on the rack over his head. He wiped the top of the bar in front of where I'd sat. "Alex is upstairs," he said. "Passed out on my couch, with Raz."

"Passed out?"

He nodded, cracking a smile. "She had a few drinks." He leaned with his hands on the bar. "Looks to me like she wanted to let loose, maybe spend a night not worrying about everything you two are dealing with."

"I can't blame her," I said. "I know I could use one."

Billy grabbed the bottle of Jack, with a look that turned serious. "You think maybe you've bitten off more than you can chew?" He poured me a shot and slid the glass across.

"I wouldn't say more than I could chew, but—"

179

"Well, is it more than you'd expected? Or would've somehow been easier?"

"What's that supposed to mean?" I said. I guess I was getting defensive. "You don't think I can handle this?"

Billy put up his hands, as if to tell me to relax. "Let me finish, okay? All I'm saying is maybe you need to alter your approach. I know how you've been hesitant to stand on the same side of the line with Alex's friends over at the sheriff's office. But maybe you should consider, I don't know, taking that wall down you like to put up, maybe give what's his name... Mike Stone? Maybe give him a chance, see if there's a way the two of you can—"

"Okay, I see what's going on here." I stared back at him. "How long did Alex have your ear? Because the things you're saying sound like they'd come straight out of her mouth. Is that the story? Did she ask you to say something to me?"

He appeared hesitant to admit anything, but I knew both Alex and Billy well enough to see through whatever was on their minds. He shrugged. "She might've said a couple of things while she was at the bar."

"You should know better," I said. "She trusts law enforcement a lot more than I do." I finished what was in my glass and left some cash on the bar, heading for the stairs to Billy's office.

Billy watched me go around the bar. "Where are you going?"

"To see how she's doing."

I went and opened the door. Raz barked and charged me before he could see it was me.

Alex jumped up from the couch, her eyes wide, breathing heavy, and had her gun raised and pointed at me.

"Whoa," I said, my hands up in front of me. "It's just me."

Raz sat, tail wagging.

Alex placed the Glock down on the cushion next to her and leaned forward, rubbing her face with her hands. "What time is it?"

"After midnight."

She fixed her hair, tying it with a band behind her head.

"How was your get-together?" I said.

She stood up from the couch, slapped her hand against her thigh, and Raz ran toward her. "It was nice to catch up. Chris didn't stick around long, had an early shift."

I was glad to hear it.

"Are you really sleeping here tonight?"

Alex looked at the couch, shaking her head. "I can't believe I even took a nap on it. But I'm so tired."

"You haven't stopped," I said.

She nodded, looking over at me. "I know. Neither have you." She grabbed her throat. "I need a drink."

"A drink? I thought maybe you had enough?"

"I don't mean alcohol. I'm dehydrated. I need water."

"Do you want to go down? Billy's cleaning up."

"Is there anyone else at the bar?"

"There's nobody at all." I said, "Just Billy. It's closed."

Alex said, "I'm not even sure how long I've been asleep." She patted her pockets and looked at the couch. "Where'd I put my phone?"

She reached down and lifted the blanket that'd been rolled up in the corner. Her phone dropped onto the floor, and she picked it up, looking at the screen. "I guess I missed some calls."

"I called," I said. "But didn't leave a message."

She tapped the screen. "Mike left a message." She started to listen, her eyes widening, then tapped the screen again, and put it on speaker so I could hear it:

One witness claimed there was a white pickup driving around earlier in the evening. I'm sure you already know, of course, Henry was there." The message went quiet for a moment, then Mike continued. *I don't know if you need to share this with him, but Henry might've been right. It's not looking as much of a suicide as we first suspected. Someone else might've been in there with her.*" Again, the message went quiet. "*I hope you're okay. Give me a call when you get this.*"

Alex hung up and kept her eyes down on the phone. "What is he talking about?"

"Same thing I'd called you about. But I didn't leave a message? It's Kayla Morton. She's dead."

I told her everything that had happened, and how the entire night had gone, starting with the moment I showed up outside Kayla's apartment.

"Mike practically said I was crazy when I said someone was involved. Of course, they assumed she'd jumped. At the time, there was no evidence of anyone being in her apartment, according to the sheriff's office." I walked to the window and looked out into the darkness, my crooked reflection in the window. "Why would he tell you not to tell me? What's wrong with him? It's like he's afraid to give me even an ounce of credit... or respect. Whatever it is, I just don't get it."

We walked toward the stairs, and I stopped to let Alex and Raz go down ahead of me.

"What did your friend have to say about Theresa Thompson? Anything else besides what was in the reports?"

Alex stopped at the bottom of the stairs. "He said he'd look into it as much as he can, but he said that the details are so thin, it's almost as if it wasn't heavily investigated. As you saw in the report, there were no signs of foul play."

We walked toward the quiet bar.

Billy had already dimmed the lights and turned off the TV. He walked through the swinging door from the kitchen, keys in his hand. He gave Alex a crooked smile. "How are you feeling?"

She shrugged with a small grin. "Can I get a glass of water?"

Billy got her a pint filled with ice water and placed it in front of her. As soon as she finished, we followed him through the kitchen and out the back. He set the alarm and locked the door.

"Where are you staying?" he said, leaning down to pet Raz. "You're all welcome to stay at my house. It's safe. I can promise you that."

"I think Raz and I will be okay at my house." But then she looked at the Jeep. "Oh, I forgot we only have the Jeep between us."

"Why don't we go to the boat?" I said. "It's two minutes away, and you're in no condition to drive."

She didn't look like she knew what to do. But she didn't have much of a choice. "Come on, you and Raz can have the bed again."

Billy walked to his Lexus and opened the door. "The invitation stands," he said. "I have plenty of space."

"We'll be all right," I said, speaking for Alex when I wasn't sure I should.

He stepped into his car. "You should plan to come over in the morning and pick up your car. It's all ready for you."

I watched Billy turn from the lot and disappear down the street, but then noticed someone else's car parked in front of the restaurant. Alex had already gotten into the passenger side of her Jeep, although I started walking toward what looked like a red Volkswagen Jetta. But as I got closer, the car took off. It was too dark for me to see the plates, and there was no chance I could see who was behind the wheel.

I ran back to the Jeep and jumped in, starting the engine, and looked into the back seat. "Where's Raz?"

Alex turned and saw he wasn't there. "Raz?" She looked around. "Raz? Come on, boy."

Luckily, he was fine. He was doing his business, over near the bushes at the back of the lot.

Alex helped him up into the Jeep, and he slipped into the back where he lay down.

Chapter 26

ALEX AND I DROVE around the area looking for the red Volkswagen for a good twenty minutes before turning toward the marina. But as I pulled into the parking lot, it hit me. I cut the wheel and spun the Jeep around and drove off.

Alex gave me a look, like I was crazy. "What are you doing?"

"Going to River's Edge."

"Can you please tell me why?" she said. "I don't want another drink, even if they're still open."

"They close at two. Young crowd."

It was 1:47 on the clock when we pulled up to the front of the restaurant. I drove through the back parking lot and looked for a red Jetta but didn't see it. "I'm almost certain there was one in the parking lot, when I got into it with Mason." There weren't a lot of cars in the lot, and I pulled out onto the street, backing into an empty parking space by the front door.

I started to step out of the Jeep, and Alex said, "Didn't you promise Brian you wouldn't go in his restaurant anymore?"

"I don't have a choice," I said. "I want to know who owns a red Jetta. Someone was clearly watching us, and..."

Alex stepped out onto the sidewalk. "You wait here, and I'll go in and find out if anyone knows whose it is."

I watched her walk up to the front door and go inside without looking back, then I got inside the Jeep and looked through the window. Lydia didn't appear to be behind the bar, but Alex walked up to the bar and said something to the bartender. She gave him a nod, then walked out the front door and stepped into the Jeep. "It was Lydia."

"Lydia?" I said, somewhat surprised but not completely.

I shifted the Jeep into drive and looked once more through the window. "She wasn't there?"

"The bartender said she doesn't work there anymore."

I wondered why. I glanced at Alex but didn't say a word.

"What about Mason? Did you see him?"

Alex shook her head and checked on Raz, reaching back to pet him. "I didn't recognize anyone there. It doesn't mean Mason wasn't there."

I stopped at a red light. "You seem to be all right," I said, "for someone who had too much to drink."

"Who told you I had too much to drink? I only had two." I could feel her staring at me. "I was exhausted, that's all."

"You passed out on Billy's dirty couch."

"I don't have to be hammered to take a nap, you know."

I laughed. "Sorry, I guess I just assumed..."

187

She held her gaze for another moment, then turned, looking out the passenger window as we crossed over the St. Johns, on the Main Street Bridge.

Alex said, "Aren't you going to tell me where we're going?"

"To find Lydia. She lives in the Springfield area, off North Liberty."

• • • • ●•● • ● •• •

The old two-story house had dark-brown siding and was smaller, compared to some of the other houses we'd passed. There were no lights on inside or outside the house, and I killed the Jeep's lights when I pulled into the driveway.

"We have no idea if the car at Billy's was hers," Alex said. "You sure we should knock on her door at this time? It's morning."

We both got out and walked to the front door. But Alex stopped and looked toward the back of the house. "There's a garage back there," she said.

I could barely see it. I walked past Alex, to the garage, looking inside through the windows.

The old garage's interior was a mess. There was so much junk, a car would never fit.

"If it was her car," I said, "it's not here."

We walked back toward the front of the house. But headlights shined on us. A car pulled into the driveway and stopped behind the Jeep.

"It's the Jetta," I said, seeing Lydia behind the wheel, staring at us through the windshield. The reverse lights lit up the end of the driveway, and Lydia squealed the tires, backing out onto the street.

I ran across the grass and into the street, stopping in front of her car. Unless she wanted to run me over—there was a chance she would—her only option was to go in reverse.

I could feel the heat of the engine on my legs.

Lydia turned in her seat, the reverse lights brightening up the road. But Alex was standing behind her, taking the chance Lydia wouldn't do something foolish.

The reverse lights went off, the engine still running.

Alex walked to the driver's side and knocked on the window. She acted like a cop, and I'm not sure Lydia knew if she was or wasn't one. "Turn off your engine," Alex said.

Lydia did as she was told, then sat in her seat, gazing toward her lap.

Alex pulled open the door, and Lydia looked up at her. "I'm sorry."

I walked over and stood with Alex. "Can you tell me what you were doing at Billy's Place earlier?"

"I'm sorry. I... I wanted to talk to you. That's all."

I said, "Then why'd you take off?"

She shrugged, looking from me to Alex. "I changed my mind. I shouldn't get involved."

"Involved in what?" I said, although I had a general idea what she meant.

189

She looked toward her house. "I knew I should've told you, but I guess I wasn't sure it mattered." She said to Alex, "Are you a cop?"

"No," Alex said, and left it at that.

I said, "Lydia? Can you please tell us what it was you wanted to tell me?"

She said, "I heard something. And I'm not sure what it all meant. It was a little while ago, but I started to think about it after some of the things that've happened around here." Lydia appeared nervous and maybe scared. "I heard about Kayla."

"You knew her?" I said.

"Not personally. But John had mentioned her a couple of times."

I looked into Lydia's car. "Where are your keys?"

"In the ignition."

"Let's get this thing out of the road. "I slid behind the wheel, adjusting the seat back so I could fit. Lydia's legs were half the length of mine.

I moved the car into the driveway, and Alex and Lydia walked up together as I stepped out.

"Okay, Lydia," I said. "No more games. Start talking."

She said, "I overheard Mr. Mason talking on the phone a few weeks ago. I was with Brian, when we were over at his house."

"You're talking about Roy Mason?" I said. "Brian's father?"

She nodded. "He had no idea I was listening."

"What'd you hear?" Alex said, clearly as anxious as I was for Lydia to tell us what she'd heard.

"It was before... before any of this happened. Before John died." She stopped herself, her arms folded like she was cold. "I'm almost certain he was talking to John. I wasn't sure who it was at the time, but the more I've thought about it—"

"Lydia," I said, growing more impatient as she dragged us along. "Please tell us what you heard."

"Mr. Mason told whoever it was he was talking to that Nate Ryan would have to be dealt with." She looked me in the eye. "Nate is John's stepson. I'm the one who told him to call you, and gave him the number off your card."

I nodded. "He did call me."

"You sure you heard him right?" Alex said. "He said Nate would have to be dealt with?"

Lydia seemed hesitant at first. "Well, I guess I'm not one hundred percent certain. He may have said Nate had to be spoken to. But I think I had it right, the way I said it the first time."

"Was that *it*?" I said.

She shook her head. "No. I heard him say, if he knows what happened, then it's up to you—the person, I think John, on the other end—to fix the problem. Mr. Mason said that if he didn't, he'd have to be looking over his shoulder the rest of his life."

Alex said, "So you really have no way of knowing if it was John on the other end." She glanced at me, giving me a look like she wasn't sure she was ready to buy the story.

Lydia said, "I didn't know at the time. With Nate coming around again lately, talking about his mother and John's death..." She turned toward me. "And then you show up asking questions, I started to think about what I'd heard that night, and it all sort of adds up." She pushed her hair back. "I'm sorry. I knew I shouldn't have said anything."

"No, it's okay," I said, thinking. "But, can you tell me what Nate wanted to talk to you about?"

"Just that he wished he'd talked to John."

"Nate said he wished he talked to John? Did he tell you *why*?"

Lydia shook her head. "I think Nate's a good kid, and he wouldn't hurt anyone, if you think he had anything to do with what happened to John."

I wondered if what Lydia told us had any legs. I thought about Roy, going out of his way to make sure I knew John was his good friend. "Have you heard from Nate?"

Lydia shook her head, and the three of us stood quiet for a moment. Raz had his head hanging over the side of the Jeep, watching us.

I nodded toward Lydia's house. "Why don't you go ahead and get inside; get yourself some sleep."

She nodded, then walked to her car. "I'll move my car, so you can get your Jeep out of the driveway." She opened the car door.

"Lydia," I said. "What happened at the River's Edge? I heard you're not working there anymore?"

"I guess not," she said. "Brian and I had a fight."

Chapter 27

I'M NOT SURE I was fully awake as I stepped down off the boat early in the morning, the sun barely over the horizon. I grabbed my chair and set it down on the dock, sitting down, wishing I could go below to my own bed and get an hour of sleep. But of course Alex and Raz were down there again, although I appreciated nobody showed up on the boat looking to fight me.

It had only been a few hours since we'd gotten back from Lydia's house, and I was exhausted. There was a chill in the morning air, but it was comfortable. I leaned my head back and closed my eyes.

I felt a hand on my shoulder and opened them to bright sunshine and warmth I hadn't felt a moment earlier. The fact was, it wasn't a moment earlier when I'd closed my eyes, although it seemed it.

Alex said, "You slept in your chair? All night?"

"No. I woke up, thinking I'd sit out and watch the sun rise." The sky was bright blue. "I guess I missed it." Looking at my watch, I saw two hours had gone by.

I stood up from the chair, my neck feeling stiff.

"I could hear your snoring from your bed down below," she said. "The way your head was back on the chair. You're lucky you didn't fall in the river."

I wiped my face with both hands and folded up the lawn chair. I was hungry.

Alex said, "I'm going to walk Raz, if you want to come? Maybe we can go out and get breakfast somewhere?" She gazed at Raz as he plopped on the dock at her feet.

"There's a little breakfast place down in San Marco. Beach Diner. Got some tables outside. They allow dogs."

"San Marco?" she said, with a curious tone.

I nodded. "From there, we can go see Michelle."

• • • • • ● ● ● • • •

I was driving the Jeep, heading down 17 and over the Main Street Bridge, into San Marco. I was supposed to go by Billy's to get the car he had for me, but I decided to go there later.

Alex's phone rang as we turned onto Atlantic Boulevard.

"It's Mike," she said, but didn't pick it up right away.

I said, "Aren't you going to answer it?"

She stared at the screen, like she was thinking, then answered. "Hi, Mike." She nodded. "Yeah, everything's okay. Yes." She listened, then looked at me. "I'm actually with him right now."

By the look on her face, I knew it was more than a social call.

"Raz and I stayed on Henry's boat." She stayed quiet, listening. "Yes, I'll let him know. Thank you, Mike." She hung up and said, "He has the life insurance policy you told him you were meeting Kayla for."

"Oh no," I said. "That's not good."

"Why not?"

"Because we need it."

She looked at me, confused. "Why do you think he called? He wants you to see it. I don't know how many times I have to tell you this, but Mike's not a bad guy. The truth matters to him, as much as it does to you."

• • • • • • • • • • •

The waitress at the Beach Diner came over to our outdoor table with barely a smile. She was young and pretty with long, brown hair. I noticed how red her eyes were. I guessed she'd been crying.

"Good morning," she said, her voice cracking. "My name's Cary."

I pulled my sunglasses down from my face. "I'm sorry if this is none of my business to ask, but are you all right?"

Alex and I stared at her, waiting.

A tear slipped out of the corner of her eye, and she wiped it with her hand. "I'm so sorry," she said, trying to force out a grin. "It hasn't been a good morning for me." She spotted Raz. "He's cute."

"Hey, we're cool," I said. "If you need to get something off your chest? We're all ears."

She looked from me to Alex. "That's nice of you, but..."

"Okay, I won't pry," I said. "I'll just have a coffee. Black."

Alex ordered green-and-peach tea and watched Cary walk away. "Poor girl looks so upset. Something must've happened."

"Or maybe she hates her job," I said. "Or her boss is a jerk."

Cary came out within a few minutes and placed our drinks on the table. The tears in her eyes hadn't cleared.

Alex said, "Are you sure you're okay?"

She nodded, sniffling. "I really am sorry about this. I just found out a friend of mine died last night."

Alex and I both said sorry at the same time.

"You might've heard about it. It was on the news."

"Do you mind if I ask what happened?" I said.

She shook her head, trying to gather herself. "She lives in those new apartments, by the St. Johns Town Center."

I knew, without even having to ask. "The apartments. The Jax?"

Cary looked at me and nodded.

"Kayla Morton?" I said. "She's a friend of yours?"

Cary's expression changed. "Do you know her?"

I nodded and straightened out in my seat. "I'm sorry," I said, but didn't go into the fact I was the one right there when her body fell ten feet from where I stood.

Cary said, "I feel awful about it. Life gets busy, you know? It's been a long time since I saw her, but... when something like this happens, I wish I'd called her, to see how she was doing. I had no idea..." She wiped her cheek.

"When was the last time you saw her?" I said.

"Funny, but it was right here. She acted kind of strange, to be honest. She didn't know I worked here, so I guess it was weird for both of us." She pushed out a crooked smile. "I didn't think I'd be waiting at a diner, when my friends are working real jobs, and—"

"Any job is a real job," I said, although I'm not sure it's what she needed to hear. "Was it recently? That she was here?"

Cary nodded. "She was with this old guy. I don't mean an old man or anything, like it wasn't her grandfather or anything. But he was older, you know? I couldn't hear everything they were saying, but she seemed upset. I got the feeling he was being mean to her, acting like a jerk. After she left, I'd called her to make sure everything was okay." She sniffled. "But I never talked to her. She didn't call me back."

I pulled out my phone and turned it toward Cary. "Is this the man she was with?" I showed her a picture of John Thompson.

Cary stared at the image on my phone and shook her head. "That's John Thompson," she said.

"You know him?" I said.

She nodded. "She wasn't here with him."

"Are you sure?"

She hesitated a moment, then nodded. "I know it wasn't him."

"And how do you know John Thompson?" I said.

Cary leaned down, toward me. "He was..." She stopped, like she was afraid to continue.

"He was *what*?" Alex said.

"He was... I don't know. I wouldn't say he was her boyfriend, but..." She kept her voice low. "Kayla was sleeping with him."

"With John Thompson?" I said, somewhat surprised to hear it from an alleged friend of Kayla's. But I wouldn't say I was shocked.

I said, "Makes sense."

"My other friends and I, well—I feel bad about it now—but we'd joke about how Kayla made all this money, how she'd gotten such a good job, promoted so fast. And that place where she lived, the Jax, it's pretty expensive, you know."

She turned and glanced toward the tinted glass door to the restaurant. "I should probably take your order before it gets busy. The crowds start to come in around this time."

"I just want to make sure. You don't think it was John Thompson she was here with?"

Cary shook her head. "I know what John Thompson looks like. But this man with Kayla was bigger. He had white hair."

She paused, thinking. "He had a limp when he got up. But, just to be clear, I don't think they were together or anything. I mean, in any kind of a romantic way. At least I *hope* not. But I guess you never know."

I said to Alex, "Do you have a picture of Roy Mason on your phone?"

Alex tapped the screen and turned it toward Cary. "Is this the man who was with Kayla?"

She nodded with a bit of enthusiasm. "Did you say Roy Mason? That sounds right. Now that you mention it, he introduced himself to me, acted like he was someone important."

Chapter 28

WE TURNED INTO MICHELLE Thompson's neighborhood, and I'd expected to drive straight through the gate, considering I'd made a pretty good acquaintance of Mickey. But he walked out from the brick guardhouse and stood in front of the Jeep, so I'd stop.

"Morning, Henry," he said, walking over to my side. "Here to see Mrs. Thompson again?" He tipped his hat to Alex, then shifted his eyes to Raz, in the back seat.

I said, "Can I get through?"

Mickey shook his head. "She's not home. Left, oh, maybe twenty minutes ago." He looked around as if making sure nobody was listening, then leaned in close to me. "Between you and me, she's out with a friend of Mr. Thompson's."

"Do you know him?"

Mickey nodded. "I know just about every person who comes in and out of this place. Name's Roy Mason. Nice gentleman,

I suppose." He peered at me over his sunglasses. "Was she expecting you this morning?"

"Michelle? Not exactly," I said, being honest with the man. "But I wish I'd gotten here twenty minutes earlier. I wouldn't have minded bumping into Mr. Mason."

"Sounds like you know who he is?" Mickey said.

"Has Roy been over to see Michelle a lot lately?"

"You mean, since Mr. Thompson passed away?" He nodded. "Now, I understand a man should do whatever he can to help take care of a friend's widow, but..." He cleared his throat, looking toward the road. "I don't know. Something about him coming over here all the time doesn't sit right with me. You know what I'm saying?"

"Of course," I said.

Mickey backed away from the Jeep, clearing his throat. "I'm sorry about that. It's probably none of my business."

"Oh, I don't know if that's true, Mickey. You're the one watching out for the people who depend on you to keep them safe. It's part of your job, making sure you know who's coming in and out of this neighborhood, isn't it?"

Mickey paused, like he wasn't sure. He finally nodded. "I suppose you're right." He pulled off his hat and pushed his graying hair back on his head. "I hadn't seen much of Mr. Mason over the past couple of months. But ever since that morning, I swear the man'd been here just about every morning, to see Mrs. Thompson."

"Which *morning*?" I said. "The morning John was killed?"

Mickey nodded. "I didn't know anything of it at the time. But Roy Mason, I'm almost certain, came through here, oh, had to be sometime before nine that morning, give or take a few minutes. I mean, I assumed he was here to show his support and condolences. But after the fact, I got to thinking about it. I believe they said it all happened earlier that morning. So, I'm thinking back, I'm not sure Roy Mason knew at the time or not. But, like I said, right around nine o'clock, here he comes driving up in that old, mint-green Chevrolet truck he drives."

Alex leaned forward, so she could see Mickey outside my door. "Any idea how long Roy was here?"

Mickey shook his head. "I'm only here till eleven on Sundays. I'm sure he was still there when I left. Like I said, I didn't know nothin' of John's death at the time. Went on my way to church, made it in time for the eleven-thirty service."

"Officers must've come out to see Michelle that morning?"

He nodded. "They didn't tell me what for, at the time. I usually let them right through, of course."

I glanced at Alex in the passenger seat and shifted the Jeep into reverse. "Thanks for taking the time to talk to us, Mickey. It might not be a bad idea if you and I keep this between us, if that's all right?"

· · · ● · ● · ● · · ·

"I don't have much time," Angela said, standing in her doorway, looking out at me and Alex. She was dressed in business attire. "I need to get to the office. With everything that's happened, I'm afraid of what this is going to do to my employees."

"You remember Alex?" I said.

Angela nodded without much of an acknowledgment. She stretched her neck and looked past us, toward the Jeep. "Is that a dog in the back seat?"

Alex smiled. "That's Raz."

Angela stepped back from the door. "Please, come inside." She led us down the hall and into the kitchen at the back of the house. "Is there any news on Kayla?"

"We don't know yet," I said.

Angela held up a pot of coffee. "Would either of you like a cup?"

Alex shook her head. "No thank you."

I needed the caffeine, so Angela poured a coffee into a Thompson Insurance mug and placed it on the marble-topped island. She took a seat on the other side and gestured across from her. "Please, have a seat."

Alex and I both sat, and I said, "A lot has happened in the past twelve hours."

Angela closed her eyes and sighed, shaking her head. "It's just hard to understand why. First John. And now Kayla?"

"There's obviously a good chance the two are tied together," I said.

Angela stared at me. "And you really don't believe it was suicide? Kayla must've been under a lot of pressure. Part of that is my fault, I guess. I asked her to do so much, and—"

"I don't think it was," I said. "Honestly, I'm not sure of anything yet. But I thought you should know more about Theresa's life insurance policy. We have a contact at the sheriff's office who found it in her apartment. So I believe her plan was to give it to me."

"Do you have it with you?"

"Not yet," I said. "We'll pick up a copy this afternoon."

Angela said, "I guess I still don't understand the significance of Theresa's policy. I mean, it's been five years since her death. And now, all of a sudden..."

"Her own son has a right to see it. And I'm also hoping it could open another door for us. I think it's important to know how much John received in the settlement. You never know..."

"You never know *what*?"

I said, "For someone who was as close to John as you were, I would think you'd notice if he suddenly had an extra two million dollars, don't you think?"

Angela straightened up in her seat. "I guess I... I don't understand where this is going."

"Even if Nate deserves his share, it's important for us to know what happened to all that money. And, the truth is... the details behind Theresa's death are fairly thin."

Angela had a blank stare on her face. "What are you saying? That her death may not have been an accident?" She shook her head. "This is beginning to sound ridiculous."

"I thought so, too," I said. "But I can't help wondering if Roy and John had something to hide. And there's a chance it could have something to do with what happened to Theresa."

"You honestly think John and Roy..." She got up from the stool and walked over to the kitchen sink, dumping her coffee. She stood with her back to us, quiet, before turning. "Unless you have some sort of proof, besides coming up with some kind of wild story that barely makes any sense, then I'm—"

"Someone I spoke with overheard a recent conversation Roy had with John."

Angela leaned back against the sink, waiting.

I said, "We don't know yet, without a doubt, if it was John on the other end. But the person who told me believes Roy said John's name. And Nate's name was mentioned, too."

"What is that supposed to mean? So *what*, if they had a conversation. I don't—"

"It was somewhat of a threat, coming from Roy."

Angela folded her arms. "Who told you this?"

I stood from the island. "Do you know Lydia? Brian Mason's girlfriend? Or, *ex*-girlfriend? She was over there with Brian, but at the time when she first heard it, she didn't think much of it. But then as things started to add up after John's death... Nate disappearing, and now Kayla."

Angela said, "Are you going to tell me what she heard?"

206

"She heard Roy tell whoever it was on the other end—likely, John—that he had to take care of Nate before it was too late."

Angela walked toward us. "Before *what's* too late? And how does she have any idea what he actually meant?"

"I don't know. Not yet. And we have no way of knowing if he meant to take care of Nate in a harmful way, or maybe take care of him. I was thinking it could be that Roy was telling John to pay him the money that potentially belonged to Nate."

"And why would Roy be telling John this? It doesn't make sense."

Alex said, "Like Henry said, it could be that Roy and John had something to hide."

Angela was quiet, leaning on the island with a downcast expression. "I'm sorry. I guess I'm not sure how this all ties into what happened to John."

I gave Angela a moment to take in what I was telling her. "We stopped at Beach Diner early this morning, and as luck would have it, the waitress turned out to be a friend of Kayla's. She told us Kayla had been in there recently. And do you want to guess who she was with?"

Angela shook her head.

I said, "Roy Mason."

She gasped. "Oh no. Please don't tell me you think Kayla was sleeping with—"

"No," I said. "I don't think so. But, well... I don't know how else to put this so it doesn't sound as bad as it is, but according to this young woman, John and Kayla were sleeping together."

Angela held her gaze on me, the shock in her face hard to hide. She turned from us and walked back to the sink, facing the window. "I can't believe it," she said, turning around. "He promised me, he'd never—"

"You mean, you actually talked about it?" I said.

Angela paused. "I told him what a big mistake it would be."

"But you didn't know there was something between them?" Alex said.

She shook her head. "Don't ask me why, but I trusted the man. I figured, after all we'd already been through, he wouldn't have a reason to lie to me." She rubbed her face with both hands. "Is it too early for me to have a drink?"

"I know there's a lot to digest," I said. "Probably more than you were expecting when we showed up. But with all I've told you so far, I'm going to have to dig deeper into what was going on with Roy and John. I was thinking, perhaps, I can look at whatever you have, related to his business? His policies? Including any claims he had over the past few years? You never know what we could find," I said.

"What exactly would you be looking for?" Angela said.

"I don't know. Anything out of the ordinary, I guess." I thought for a moment. "Can you give me access to whatever files are related to Roy's businesses?"

"You're not trying to say Roy was responsible for John's death, are you?"

I looked back at her but didn't have an answer.

She stepped from the sink and sat at the island, quiet for a handful of seconds. "You should go ahead and talk to Eric. Before Kayla was hired, he's the one who worked with John, and was involved in Roy's account."

• • • ● • ● • • •

I was at the desk on Alex's laptop, in her living room, while she had gone to take a shower. The search results for Roy Mason were filled with articles about the various businesses he'd owned over the years. His parent company was called Mason Industries, the developer on a number of properties throughout Jacksonville, including some on Amelia Island and a handful in other areas in the northeastern part of Florida. Most of his work, outside of a couple of residential developments, seemed to be commercial. He'd even developed two golf courses.

It wasn't until I clicked through to the third page of search results on Google that an article in the *Florida Times-Union* caught my eye, about a fire nearly seven years earlier that took down a condominium development.

It turns out Roy was involved in the development, although it wasn't Roy's main company, Mason Industries. The business was called the RJM Corporation. His wife, Joanna, was involved, which is perhaps where the "J" came from, in the name.

The company was dissolved soon after the fire.

I turned from the desk as Alex came down the stairs and into the room. She wiped at her hair with a towel, then turned and pointed to the back of her head. She smiled. "I'm not supposed to get it wet, but look: my bald spot's filling in!"

"I noticed earlier," I said. "You can hardly tell." I pointed to the laptop's screen. "Look what I found."

She leaned from behind me, her arms resting on the back of the chair.

"Roy Mason, and apparently his wife, at the time, developed condominiums out on Route 10, west of the city, about seven years ago. The whole building burned to the ground overnight, while it was still under construction."

"Does it say how it happened?"

"It was under investigation for arson at the time of the article. I haven't searched any deeper yet."

"If it's the part of town I'm thinking it is, it never turned into what they'd hoped. He was probably better off with insurance money."

We both looked at each other, as if Alex had hit the nail on the head.

I said, "Don't you think Angela would've mentioned something about this, when I asked her about Roy?"

Alex nodded, then walked out of the room.

I got up and followed her into the kitchen. "We need to talk to Roy. Maybe there's nothing to it, but—"

"Do you really think he's going to tell you *anything* at this point?"

"What about Chris?" I said. "Have you heard anything else from him, about Theresa Thompson?"

Alex shook her head. "He's trying to see what else he can find out, without anyone knowing what he's up to."

I looked out the window, toward the driveway. "What about the officer who wrote up the initial report? Can't he—"

"Chris said he retired. And he said he was young, not even thirty-five."

"You mean, when he retired?"

Alex nodded.

"Did he say if he's still a cop somewhere else?"

"We didn't get into it that much." Alex walked out of the kitchen and came back a few moments later, a manila folder open in front of her. "It says right here. The officer's name is Paul Krueger."

Chapter 29

Rosie's Pub was rocking for a weekday afternoon. Most of the stools were taken, and the five pool tables were all in use. Music cranked over the speakers for the mixed crowd, the majority of which looked like middle-aged salesmen, without much business to worry about. The handful of women were just the opposite, casually dressed in bikini tops with cutoff jeans, dressed for a day at the bar.

Eric appeared somewhat disheveled, seated at the far end of the bar from the entrance. His shirt was unbuttoned halfway down his chest, with a glass of booze in his hand, eyelids heavy and red.

A woman twice his age was hanging on his back, running her hand through his hair.

I thought about his brother, John, and his apparent love for younger women. From the looks of it, Eric preferred the other end of the age spectrum. He didn't appear to be paying much attention to her.

"This seat taken?" I said, sitting next to him.

He was still, with a crooked gaze, but didn't answer. He had no idea who I was.

The woman next to him smiled at me, her teeth big and whiter than they should've been, like a bad bleach job, although not as bad as the one on her head.

He pushed her hand away from him. "Okay, get out of here, will you?" His eyes met mine again, but it still hadn't registered with him who I was.

"I heard you might be here," I said, my eyes on the bartender, trying to get her attention.

Eric cracked a smile, his eyes opening like he'd come back to life. "Hey, I know you," he said, and his happy, drunken expression morphed into a frown. "What are you doing here?"

"Just stopping by for a drink," I said.

He squinted his eyes, although they were already half closed to begin with. "I've never seen you in here before." He waved for the bartender. "Hey, sweetie, come over here, will you?"

She walked over, and Eric said to her, "You ever see Magnum in here before?"

"Magnum?" She turned her eyes to me. "Is that really your name?"

"No," I said. "But I'll take a Jack Daniels, with rocks."

Eric tapped his glass. "Hey, fix me another one, too." He pointed at me with his thumb, a crooked smile on his face "Put it on *his* tab."

The bartender picked up Eric's empty glass, then he reached out to shake my hand. "I'm Maryanne."

"Henry."

Maryanne was attractive. Maybe she was *too* attractive to be working in a dive like Rosie's Pub.

She gave me a nice smile and started to walk away.

"Do me a favor," I said. "Just two ice cubes."

She gave me a look over her shoulder and nodded, continuing down the bar.

I said to Eric, "So, what's your story?"

"What's my story? What kind of question is that?" He repeated what I'd said under his breath, shaking his head: "*What's your story...*"

"Too hard a question for you?" I said.

He shrugged. "I'm trying to relax, man, having a few drinks. In case you forgot, I've had a lot happen in my life the last few weeks."

Maryanne came back and put our drinks down on the bar. She kept her hand on my glass for a moment longer and looked me in the eye. "Two cubes." She walked away but stopped. "I expect a good tip for all the extra-hard work."

Eric leaned into me, his hot liquor-breath burning the hairs on my face. "Dude, you're in here two minutes, you got the hottest bartender in Jax all over you?"

I picked up my glass. "All over me? All she did was pour me a drink."

He slouched over the bar, his arms folded in front of him.

"Hey, let me start off by saying I'm sorry about Kayla. I don't know how well you two got along, but—"

"Kayla was good people," he said. "She treated me all right. Better than a lot of people in that office." He faced me. "And that includes my own brother." He picked up his drink, holding it near his lips. "John would treat me like a piece of garbage, and Kayla'd speak up for me. Tell him to lay off me." He straightened in his seat and sipped his drink.

"What're you drinking?" I said.

"Vodka."

"Straight?"

He nodded and took another sip. "Now don't get the wrong idea. It's not that me and John didn't get along."

"Are you trying to say it was bad enough between you, you'd want to kill your own brother?"

He stood from his stool and slapped his hand down on the bar, pointing his finger at my face. "You'd better be making a joke, buddy. Because if you think..."

I grabbed his finger and bent it back, pushing it away from my face. "Do that again, I'll snap it off." I let go of his finger. "I know you didn't kill John."

He eased himself back down into his seat, not saying a word.

I said, "Has anybody from the sheriff's office come by to talk to you about Kayla?"

He nodded, rubbing his hand. "This morning. A couple officers showed up, asked some questions... said it was routine."

"What'd you tell them?"

"There wasn't anything to tell."

I said, "What can you tell me about John and Kayla?"

He stared back at me, eyebrows raised. "What are you asking?"

"Did you know they were sleeping together?"

Eric let out a short, loud laugh. "Who told you that, Magnum?" He shook his head. "Not a chance. Kayla wouldn't..." His expression dropped.

I said, "She wouldn't *what*?"

He shrugged and reached for a pretzel from the bowl in front of us. "What do *I* know; maybe they were sleeping together."

The way he talked, I got the feeling Eric had a lot of arguments with himself, inside his own head. Not really sure of himself. "I gotta go pee." He got up and walked away.

I sat with my drink and saw Maryanne turn to me, as if she thought I was watching her, giving a nod.

She said, "Would you like another one?"

"Not right now," I said. She came over, and I looked over my shoulder toward the men's bathroom. "Does Eric spend a lot of time here?"

She nodded, leaning on the bar. "I didn't know he had any friends, to be honest. He's usually here alone, and most of my customers try to avoid him."

I looked at the three men watching me from my left, with one stool between us. They all turned away at the same time

Eric returned, sat back on the stool and pointed at his glass. "I'll be ready for another soon, sweetie. Don't go anywhere."

She had a look like she was close to running out of patience with Eric. "I'm going to have to call you a cab, Eric." She winked at me. "Unless your friend here wants to give you a ride?"

I said, "No, you can go ahead and call him a cab."

Eric patted his pockets. "Uh-oh. What'd I do with my keys?" He scanned the bar, left and right, but within a few seconds seemed to forget what he was looking for.

Maryanne walked away, and I turned back to Eric, keeping my voice low. "I'd like to talk to you about Roy Mason."

"Yeah? What about?"

"You used to work with your brother, on Roy's accounts, is that right?"

"It's been a long time," he said. "Before Kayla."

"Okay, well let's see how good your memory is. Did you ever handle any insurance claims for Roy? Or any of his companies?"

Eric was about to take a sip from what was left in his glass, then stopped. He let out a cough, like maybe a piece of the pretzel had gotten stuck in his throat. He coughed for another half minute, half of the patrons at the bar gawking at him.

"He's fine," I said, and everyone went back to what they were doing.

"John and Kayla handled everything. I don't remember what I was involved with."

"Okay, then let me be a little more specific," I said. "How about that condo development that burned to the ground. I

217

assume you guys insured it? And if I do the math right, it was right around the time you were still working on the account with John."

Eric squeezed his eyes tight like a kid trying to wish something bad away. When he opened them, he stared straight ahead, toward the other end of the bar. I'm sure he wanted to be there. "You're asking about some claim from who knows how long ago? I have no idea. That fire's old news. You expect me to remember? You know how many claims go through that office every year?"

I shook my head. "No."

Eric stared at me with his bloodshot eyes and, if possible, his wheels turning.

I said, "If there was a settlement for Roy's property, then there must be documentation somewhere, correct?"

Eric rubbed his forehead. "You're giving me a headache with all these questions. I don't remember." He picked up his glass. "Even if I did, I don't have to tell you a thing."

"No, you don't," I said. "But I assure you, I'll find what I need, one way or the other. Angela will help me. I thought I'd give you the chance, before I took another avenue." I pushed my empty glass forward and stood from my seat. "And I know enough people at the sheriff's office to get them involved, if I need to. I'm sure once they start digging..." I threw a bill on the bar and started for the door.

"Wait!" he said, following me. "Are you asking me about that fire because you think this has to do with what happened to my brother?"

I pulled him toward the door, so nobody else could hear. "It might."

Eric said, "Do you think Roy—"

"I don't know yet. But if you cooperate with me..."

He paused and pulled me outside, onto the sidewalk. The sun was warm and bright, heating up the concrete.

"I made a mistake when I was working for John. I mean, I really screwed up, man. It could've ruined the whole company." He took a deep breath, shaking his head. "It was bad for everyone. That's when John lost it, on me. Big time. He was going to fire me. And Roy was even worse. I'm still surprised he didn't kill me."

I waited a moment as two men walked past us and through the entrance to the bar. "Eric, please tell me you didn't light the damn fire."

"No, it was nothing like that. I may be a screwup, but I don't..." He stopped. His eyes were already red but seemed to be glossed over. "I... I never filed for Roy's coverage. I mean, he had coverage for the property. But it was the minimum, whatever was automatic as part of his overall policy. I was supposed to push it up to the maximum allowed after I'd already gotten the property appraised. Of course, a friend of John and Roy's performed the appraisal, so it was whatever they needed it to be. But I screwed up, because I didn't file the paperwork on time. So after the fire, Roy only got a little over a million dollars."

"A million dollars?" I said. "It sounds like a lot."

Eric nodded. "The building was worth a lot more. He was expecting another three."

"I guess that's a pretty big loss. Did he do it himself?" I said. "Did Roy burn it down?"

Eric shook his head. "Oh, I don't think so. The police investigated it for arson, but nothing was ever proven. I mean, who knows for sure. Roy has plenty of his own connections at the sheriff's office."

"Well, you're still working there, so I guess John didn't put all the blame on you?"

"John covered for me. And Angela never even knew about it. But I'm not sure Roy and John—their friendship, or whatever it was—was ever the same. To this day, I still don't know why Roy didn't take his business somewhere else."

Chapter 30

PAUL KRUEGER, THE EX-COP whose name was on the police report detailing the scene of Theresa Thompson's death, took his time as he stepped out the back door of the Andrea Perrone Art Gallery, where he worked. It was before dusk, the sun just about down as he walked across the parking lot toward his rust-colored Pontiac Trans Am. There was a touch of humidity in the air, even though the temperature had cooled.

Alex and I approached him as he pulled his keys from his pocket and unlocked the driver's-side door.

"Paul Krueger?" I said.

He turned, alarmed, and cocked his arm with a closed fist, keys dangling from the door as he reached for the gun tucked into the holster on his belt.

"Whoa," I said, hands up.

Paul was young for a retired cop, although his face was not without wear. The man was built like a house, although a few inches shorter than me. The sleeves on his button-down shirt were rolled up tight around his biceps, showing off his pipes.

"Who the hell are you?" he said, looking from me to Alex.

"I'm Henry Walsh. This is Alex."

"You shouldn't sneak up on someone like that. Lucky you didn't get shot." He hadn't taken his hand from the holstered gun.

"Sorry," I said. "But we're hoping you can help us out, regarding an old case you worked on when you were with the sheriff's office."

He pulled his keys from the lock and opened the car door, lifting his foot to step inside.

I grabbed the door to keep him from closing it as he slipped behind the wheel. "Wait," I said.

But that was a mistake.

He jumped from the seat after he slammed the door open into me, coming across with his other hand, punching me in the jaw. It was jarring, to say the least, and sent me stumbling back a couple of feet.

I had my arm cocked, ready to swing, but Alex grabbed me from behind. "Don't."

Paul stepped out from behind the door, fists raised. "You want a piece of me?"

He waved me toward him, ready to go at it, bare knuckles.

I rubbed my jaw and felt around the inside of my mouth with my tongue. I could taste my own blood. I put my hands up, palms out, shaking my head. "A little hot under the collar, aren't you?"

"You don't show up, try to—"

"It's about Theresa Thompson," I said, holding my jaw. "You were the officer on the scene."

He shook his head. "Don't know nothing about it." He tried to step back into his car.

I grabbed the police report from Alex and held the paper flat against the window as he pulled on the door, slamming it closed. I yelled through the glass. "Your name's right here."

The car's engine started, doors locked, but Paul Krueger sat with his head down for a moment without looking at us. He reached for the key in the ignition, killing the motor. He sat still for another moment, then pushed open the door, and stepped out.

"Did you know her?" he said.

"Theresa?" I shook my head. "I'm a private investigator."

"You're investigating Theresa Thompson's—"

"I'm following leads on another case. But they're related."

He stared back at me, closing his door behind him. "Just because my name's on the report doesn't mean I was the only one involved." He gazed at the pavement. "I was the one who took the fall."

I gave Alex a quick glance. "Took the fall for *what*?"

He said, "Oh, I thought maybe you..." He looked around the parking lot. "I was forced to retire right around the same time I started to investigate the Theresa Thompson case. Not that there was much of one to begin with."

"Much of what?" I said. "A case?"

He nodded. "I wasn't exactly allowed to do my job the way I wanted to. And when it was determined her death was caused by an accidental fall, it didn't sit right with me. But they told me it was an accident. End of story."

"I don't understand," I said. "What do you mean, someone *told* you it was an accident?"

"My superiors." He looked at the report I was holding in my hand. "You going to tell me what this has to do with, if it's not about Theresa Thompson?"

"I'm investigating her husband's death."

"John Thompson?" He huffed, shaking his head as he gazed around the dark parking lot. "I saw they called that one an accident, too, huh? A *freak* accident, just like what they said about his wife." His eyes shifted to mine. "So let me guess—you're trying to prove it wasn't an accident? Good luck with that."

"I'm sure there's a connection. But I need some help trying to pull the pieces together."

"Well, I don't know much about what happened with Mr. Thompson, but I may be able to share a thing or two about Theresa Thompson's case."

"Whatever you can share, I'd appreciate it," I said.

He again looked around the parking lot. "You want the long version? Or the short one?"

Alex said, "How about somewhere in between?"

"Whatever you can tell us," I said.

Paul nodded, taking his time to get started. The street by the gallery buzzed with moving traffic. "They tried to make it look like I botched the investigation. Are you aware of that?"

I shook my head. "I don't know much more than what's on this report," I said.

"The thing is," he said, "I have no idea who was behind it. But nothing ever smelled right, from the moment I walked through that door, starting with the way Mr. Thompson was acting. If I'd only been allowed to keep digging." He shook his head. "The whole scene that night, it was... it was too clean. I mean, to be honest, most people'd look at it, that there was little doubt she'd simply fallen. It happens. But there was something about it, and I couldn't get it out of my mind. But there was nothing I could do."

I watched him step toward the car and lean back against it.

"Like I said, they said I made mistakes."

"Your superiors?" I said.

"My immediate supervisor, Sgt. Andy Meredith. He was the one who shut me down."

I said to Alex, "You know him?"

She shook her head.

Paul gave Alex a nod, his eyes opened wide. "You're not with the sheriff's office, are you?"

"She's not," I said.

Paul looked her over. "You look like a cop."

Alex said, "I was, at one time. But not around here."

I said, "Is he still with the sheriff's office?"

"Sergeant Meredith?" Krueger shook his head. "Killed in the line of duty. About three months after I left. Too bad. He was a nice guy." He paused. "It was never his call."

"What wasn't his call?" I said.

"Forcing me out of there." Paul watched two other security guards walk out the back door of the building, looking toward us.

One of the two, like Paul, looked like a bodybuilder. He said, "You all right over there, Paul? I thought you left?"

Paul waved them off. "We're good. Have a good evening, boys." He watched, waiting for the two men to get to their cars before he continued. "I was given a specific reason why I was forced out, but they put me in a position where I couldn't fight it. I couldn't even question it. I was told they'd help me get in with another organization, maybe in another city." With his fingers, he pulled on the chest of his shirt, where his name was stitched on one side and the word *SECURITY* was patched on the other. "Five years later, here I am... security's as close as I ever got. I turn forty next month. Any chance of a real law enforcement career is over."

Alex gave me a look, with a slight grin, and I knew what she was thinking.

Paul straightened himself out from his car, looking at me and Alex. "Something funny about that?"

I shook my head. "No, not at all. I'm not going to go into it now, but if you knew my story... you'd be surprised to hear why I know, firsthand, exactly where you're coming from. My career took a similar turn to yours. Although I was much younger at the time."

"Yeah?"

I said, "A story for another time."

The three of us stood quiet, the mood somewhat lighter for at least a couple of moments.

"So, who hired you?" Krueger said. "Thompson's wife?"

"Ex-wife," I said. "She's his business partner."

Paul said, "Angela?"

I nodded. "You know her?"

"I always wondered if she was somehow involved in the second Mrs. Thompson's death. Especially since John Thompson had left her for the second wife."

I thought for a moment, looking at the report in my hand. "Is this entire report completely inaccurate?"

"It's, say, if anything... it's incomplete. That's all. If they hadn't cut my legs off, I know I would've found something."

Alex said, "But you had no real suspects?"

He took a deep breath and followed with a loud sigh. "Technically, no. But I had my suspicions."

"John Thompson?" I said.

Paul looked at me, like I struck a nerve. "The minute I walked through the door and saw his wife lying there at the bottom of the stairs..." He shook his head. "Like I said, there was something about the way he acted. I don't know. I—"

"But they wouldn't let you continue the investigation?" Alex said.

"Sergeant Meredith pulled me in, told me to back off. At first he said there were legal issues. I knew that was bullshit. John Thompson wasn't the first husband with a lot of money and a dead wife."

"What do you mean by that?" I said. "You know how much money he had?"

Krueger shrugged. "He owned that company. Nice house. Fancy car. I never got to where I was able to look at his bank account, if that's what you're asking."

I said, "What happened to Sergeant Meredith? How was he killed?"

"Was shot point-blank, as soon as he walked through the door of his house. They said it was a B and E, and that he must've walked in on whoever was in there."

"You sound like you don't believe it?" I said.

He let out a huff, looking toward the building. "I don't know why I stick around this place. All I do is try to live my life, but I'll tell you, I'm always looking over my shoulder. I try to tell myself I'm just being paranoid, but—"

"You know you might not be," I said. I flipped over the report and looked at the second page. "John Thompson was at his friend Roy Mason's house, playing cards?"

Krueger nodded. "That's what he said."

"You talk to anyone else who was there? At the alleged card game?"

"Yeah, one other guy. I don't even remember his name. But otherwise, as I keep telling you, I wasn't allowed to go any further or question anybody else. I know it sounds crazy, but this case was never actually investigated."

"What about Roy Mason?" I said. "Do you know much about him?"

"I know he had some friends at the sheriff's office. I know his son, Brian. I mean, I don't know him personally. We steer clear of each other. I'm not even sure what he knows about this one time: Brian's got this buddy of his—a real meathead—who I had a few words with out in the parking lot of the gym we belong to. It's the same one Brian works out at. This guy was getting real aggressive with me, yelling and screaming, said I cut him off. Some of these dudes, they can't just build their muscles naturally, gotta take the needle, makes their brains all haywire."

"Steroids?" I said.

Paul Krueger nodded, rubbing his thick forearms.

I said, "Do you know this guy's name?"

"No, but I could probably get it. Hasn't been around in a long time. In fact, last time I'd say I saw him, he'd parked his truck about three inches from my door. And I know he did it on purpose. I had to crawl through the passenger side to get out, although I was tempted to smash my door into his. But I didn't want to damage my own car. This thing's a classic. And the black on white would've made it clear who did it."

"Black on white?" I said.

"Yeah." He nodded toward the Trans Am. "This guy's got this big white pickup. Big wheels, the whole—"

"Any chance it was a Ford? An F-250?"

"Yeah, that's exactly what it was."

Chapter 31

Alex turned the Jeep into the parking lot behind River's Edge Bistro, and I jumped out before she'd come to a full stop. Running toward the back of the restaurant, I crashed through the door. The adrenaline pumped through my veins, my body moving without my brain being clear enough to stop it.

I hadn't thought it through.

Brian Mason had his back to me, charging toward him, standing over the stove. And by the time he turned and realized I was there, it was too late. His eyes opened wide when I tackled him from the side and drove him into a stainless steel table and to the floor. Dishes crashed around us.

I had him pinned underneath me, and threw one punch after another, without giving him a chance to respond. "I knew it was you!" I yelled.

I didn't let up until someone grabbed my wrist from behind, holding my fist in midair over Brian's face.

Brian threw me off him, got up on his feet, and charged me like a linebacker, driving his shoulder into my stomach.

I fell back, nearly on top of the blue flames shooting up from the stove. I could feel the heat by my head.

The other man, dressed in a white bib apron with a baseball cap on his head, tried to help Brian by throwing wild punches, trying to hit me. But not a single punch connected, and I was sure he'd accidentally hit Brian in the back of the head, more than once.

I used my foot to try and push us away from the stove, but Brian wrapped his hands around my throat and tried to push me toward the flame.

I grabbed a steel pot by the handle and swung it at Brian, but with the heat and grease I felt, it slipped from my hand and crashed on the floor, splashing cold red sauce all over us. Brian tried to step around the puddle but slipped and fell to the floor, taking me with him.

As we fell, he tried to throw a punch, but I rolled out of the way before he connected. He was almost to his feet when he pivoted to find Alex standing behind him, her Glock pointed at his head.

"One more move, and I swear I'll put a bullet right through that thick skull."

The cook who was helping Brian slowly backed away and took off out of the kitchen.

Brian didn't move at first, his chest heaving with each labored breath. Raising his hands to Alex, he then reached for the stove, turning off the burner. He touched his mouth and looked at the tips of his fingers, but there was no way to tell if it was blood or sauce. He stared down at me. "You're lucky your girlfriend's around to save you again."

I reached for the top of the stainless steel table and pulled myself up on one knee. I grabbed a towel and tried to wipe the sauce covering most of my body, including my face. "I knew it was you. The whole time, I should've—"

"You knew *what* was me? You don't know shit," he said.

My breathing was heavy, trying to catch my breath. "The white truck. Your friend from the gym. It knew it was you. You sent him to kill us!"

"What friend? What white truck? What the hell are you talking about, Walsh?" His hands were still raised. "What is he talking about?"

"We know it was you," she said. "And now we can tie it all to you and your father."

Brian shook his head. "I don't have any idea what you're talking about. You're both crazy. I'm telling you—"

"Let's go," I said, pointing toward the door. "Outside."

The other cook who had tried to help Brian turned out to be a kid, although he wasn't small. "Boss, you want me to call the cops?"

"No, it's fine," he said. "Clean this place up." Brian followed me toward the door, with Alex and her Glock behind him.

I walked outside into the dark. "We can call the sheriff's office," I said. "Or you can start by talking to us, and tell me who else you're involved with. I don't care if it's your old man or not. You're both going down."

I stepped outside and held the door.

Brian stepped over the threshold. "Where are you taking me?"

Alex poked the gun into Brian's back. "Just keep walking."

We walked around to an area around the corner with two folding chairs up against the building's exterior. There was a bucket between them filled with cigarette butts.

I pushed him into one of the chairs. "Sit down."

He sat with his thick arms crossed. "You're going to pay for this, Walsh. I hope you know that."

"*I'm* going to pay for it?" I laughed. "Why don't you go ahead and give me the name of your goon driving that white truck that almost killed us? Or are you going to keep denying you had anything to do with it?" I put my foot up on the chair next to him. "Did you kill John yourself? Or was it your psycho friend from the gym?"

Brian's eyes widened. "You're serious? You think I killed John? And you call yourself a PI? You can't find a good enough reason to prove John's death wasn't an accident, so you're going to pin it on me?"

"I have a witness," I said. "He knows your buddy from the gym."

Brian stared up at me with a stupid look on his face. "What *buddy* from the gym? I don't have any idea who you're talking about. And if you don't believe me, then maybe you should go ahead and call the sheriff's office. Tell them how you're so sure you caught the guy who killed John. Go ahead. I dare you. And you can show them what kind of proof you have, which I know is nothing." He nodded toward me, his face covered in sweat.

"There were witnesses on the balcony who saw the same pickup at Kayla Morton's apartment. And Nate Ryan spotted it two days earlier, outside her building."

Brian looked up at me, shaking his head. "I'm telling you, I don't know who it is. I'd tell you if I did."

Chapter 32

I HADN'T TALKED TO Angela, and she hadn't answered her phone. She told me she'd be up all night working, but when we drove by her house, she wasn't there. Neither was her car. Alex suggested we try her office, and sure enough, as soon as we pulled in, there was Angela's Mercedes.

But Alex and I stood outside the locked building, and for twenty minutes, Angela still hadn't answered her phone.

"Should we be worried?" I said. But as the words left my mouth, I looked through the glass and into the lobby at Angela, stepping off the elevator with her phone in her hand.

She unlocked the glass door, and as soon as she saw me, her jaw dropped and her eyes widened. "Oh my—"

"It's not blood," I said. At least most of it wasn't.

I quickly filled her in on most of what went down at Brian's restaurant and some of why my clothes were stained with red tomato sauce, although I left out a fair amount of the details.

We followed Angela across the lobby and onto the elevator.

The doors closed.

"Why are you here so late?" Alex said.

Angela leaned against the rail along the back wall. "Because it's all fallen into my lap," she said. "I don't know how I'm going to keep this business afloat. With John gone, it was bad enough. But now, without Kayla, everything's already started falling through the cracks. Clients are wondering what's going to happen, and I'm not sure I have the answers."

The bell dinged, and the elevator door slid open. Angela hurried across the hall and through the doors of Thompson Insurance.

She took us into her office and sat behind her desk, slouched over it with her head in her hands. The cup of coffee on her desk appeared old, like it hadn't been touched.

"You should get some rest," I said. "We won't take a lot of your time. But this is important."

Her eyes glossed over.

I asked her if she was okay, and a tear came down her face. "You know," she said. "Very little overwhelms me. I always thought it as one of my strengths, that I'm a strong woman. Some people might say it's that I'm just cold. But I like to think I can deal with anything and everything that gets thrown at me." She let out a sigh. "I've been through a lot in my life. But this..." She shook her head. "I should've listened to everyone who told me to let it go. Leave it alone."

"Leave *what* alone?" I said.

"This. John's death. Hiring you."

I said, "Well, Angela, the truth is—"

"Where has any of it gotten me? What's the real reason I hired you?"

Alex and I looked at each other, and I wondered what exactly was on Angela's mind. "We're getting closer," I said.

She stared at me, holding her gaze. "I'm sorry, Henry. I'm afraid this was a mistake. I should have listened to those I trust."

"What are you saying?" I said. "You don't want me to continue investigating?" I shook my head. "Angela, that would be a mistake."

"Unless you have some kind of evidence at this point, I don't see why it would be." She leaned back in her chair and brushed her hair. "I'm sorry."

"The only mistake at this point would be for us to ignore what we've found so far."

"I think we should trust the sheriff's office, and let them do their job. I know they're still investigating Kayla's death, so—"

"We've got a friend over there," I said. "Well, Alex has a friend, and he's going to help us."

Angela looked puzzled. "Someone from the sheriff's office is going to help you? I don't understand. Why would—"

"We think someone over there was involved in covering up a crime that's directly tied to John's death."

Angela sat forward in her chair and propped her elbows on the desk. "Someone at the sheriff's office had something to do with John's death?"

"Well, not exactly. But it looks like there was cover-up, concerning Theresa's death."

"*John's* Theresa?" she said. She tried to say more, but words didn't come out.

"I'm afraid there were likely a handful of people involved. Not just inside the sheriff's office, but—"

"Did John kill Theresa?" Angela shook her head. "I can't... I don't believe it. There's no way. I mean, John had his faults, but—"

"Angela, please. That's why I was hesitant to tell you any of this. We don't have all the answers yet. I can't say whether or not John had something to do with what happened to her." I stood up from the chair. "I'm asking you to trust me, and give us a little more time. We're too close to walk away."

"So I'm clear," Angela said, "You believe Theresa's death is somehow connected to what happened to John? And if you figure out what really happened to her, it'll help us get to what really happened to John? Assuming it wasn't an accident, as the sheriff's office has been adamant about since the beginning?"

I nodded. "But I need something from you."

She seemed hesitant at first, then slowly nodded. "Like what?"

"I need you to tell me everything you know about Roy Mason's insurance claim after the fire that burned down his development seven years ago. What can you tell me about the settlement?"

239

Angela was still. "I don't... I'm not sure I know what you're asking. Do you want to know how much he received? I wouldn't know. Not off the top of my head. I mean, Roy had a handful of claims and settlements over the years."

I said, "There must be a way for you to look it up, no? I can't imagine all of his settlements had to do with a development he owned, burning to the ground?"

"I wasn't really involved in that one. Or, most of them, for that matter. But I do remember when it happened, and how devastated Roy was at the time."

"I understand they found it *not* to be arson?" I said.

Angela nodded. "I believe what happened was the hardwood installers left a hot sanding machine in a closet overnight, next to a bucket of polyurethane. That's what the fire marshal had found."

Alex leaned forward in her chair. "How come you weren't involved?"

"I think I mentioned to you both that John took care of Roy's book of business. John always left me out of the loop when it came to Roy's policies."

"Why?" I said.

"I don't know. I guess because Roy was John's client from day one. And his friend. I think Roy liked it that way, and John assured him very few people were aware of whatever handshake deals those two put together. But I'll admit to you now, it was a mistake. We should've been smarter about it."

"But you said Kayla was involved in it, wasn't she?"

"With Roy's policies?" Angela nodded. "More than I ever was. I guess, somehow, John and Roy both believed they could trust her."

"But they couldn't trust you?" Alex said.

Angela didn't respond, and I waited, hesitant to continue. I still had it in the back of my mind she knew more than she was letting on.

"We spoke to Eric," I said. "And he admitted to me he screwed up Roy's policy, losing Roy quite a bit of money."

"Eric told you that?" she said. "What else did he say? How *much* money?"

"A few million. He said it was a mistake, but obviously a costly one. I can't say for sure I believe him, but Eric said when that condo development burned down, Roy's company ended up with a settlement worth a quarter of what it was supposed to be."

Angela shook her head, a look on her face like she was having trouble believing it. "John would never let such a mistake happen. He would never leave Eric in charge of something like that, without double-checking that he did everything the way John would expect."

I said, "I'm telling you what Eric said. The man was practically crying in his drink, telling me about it. The thing is, it sounded to me like John kept the whole thing purposely hidden from you."

Angela stared back at me. "If what you're saying really happened, Roy would've come in here screaming. You think he'd just let something like that go?" She shook her head. "You don't know Roy."

"But what if John got him to keep quiet, and found a way to make it up to him?"

Angela laughed. "Make it up to him, how? We didn't have two pennies to rub together back then. I guess, maybe if Roy had someone sue us, we could've had it covered. But clearly, that never happened."

I said, "You don't believe it?"

"It's not you. I'm not so sure I'd bank on whatever came out of Eric's mouth. He's known for telling stories."

Alex was staring at me.

I said to Angela, "What if Theresa's life insurance policy—worth exactly two million dollars—was enough to get Roy at least *most* of the money he was owed?"

Angela lifted the lid on her laptop and typed on the keyboard, her eyes on the screen. I wasn't sure she'd heard what I'd said, since she hardly reacted to my theory. She continued tapping the keyboard, then furiously tapped a single key numerous times with one finger. "What's going on? I can't access the details of Roy's policies!"

"Why not?"

She continued tapping the same key. "It's locked. Someone must have locked it."

"Like who?" I said.

"Maybe John, or Kayla, if I can't get in there to see it." She typed again, hammering the keys harder with her painted nails.

"There's more," I said, sitting back in the chair across from her. "Theresa's life insurance policy was changed seven months before her death. It went from one million dollars to a two-point-five-million-dollar policy."

Angela closed her eyes, because she knew exactly what it meant.

I said, "With the money from Theresa's policy, it's possible John's debt to Roy was taken care of, by almost the exact amount Roy lost on his settlement."

Chapter 33

ALEX NUDGED ME WITH her elbow, both of us looking up from the bench at Mike Stone, walking toward us, wearing a baseball hat low on his head, dark sunglasses over his eyes. We'd been at Friendship Fountain, waiting for him for over thirty minutes.

He stopped in front of us, a cigarette hanging from his mouth, looking down at me over the top of his sunglasses. "I don't like the idea of this," he said. "Just so we're clear."

"You don't like the idea of what?" I said. "That we're going to need your cooperation?"

Mike removed his sunglasses, his eyes squinted. "*You're* going to need *my* cooperation?" He laughed, slipping his glasses back over his eyes. "As usual, you've got it backward."

Alex said, "All Henry meant, was—"

"Let me tell you what the deal is," Mike said. "I'm an officer of the law. I'm not some part-time security guard who took an online course so he could play private investigator." He pointed his finger at his chest. "I'm the one who'll be expecting *your* cooperation. Your *full* cooperation." He took a drag from his cigarette and blew a stream of smoke straight at me. "Do you understand me, Walsh?"

I wanted to rip the cigarette right from the guy's mouth and flick it in his face. But I kept my cool. There was no way around it; I needed his help. "Whatever you need, Detective."

Alex looked like she wanted to say something, standing from the bench, but kept quiet. I had hoped she would've at least tried to stick up for me, tell Stone what he could do with that cigarette.

"That's good," is all Mike said. "Now, tell me what you've got." He looked at his watch. "I don't have much time."

We went into detail and told Mike everything Alex and I had learned over the past few days, and how the web was more tangled than we'd ever imagined. We asked him about Paul Krueger.

"Pretty decent guy. Not a bad cop. At least *I* thought so. But something went wrong. We weren't in the same division. In fact, I was in a financial crimes unit when I'd first started, so I didn't know much about what happened or why he abruptly retired from the force. From what I've always heard, he wasn't as clean as he should've been."

"Clean?" I said. "In what way?"

Mike pulled another cigarette from his pack and stuck it in his mouth. "Paul drank a lot and might've gotten into some trouble. But whatever happened was kept under wraps. It wasn't like he got the gold watch or anyone threw a big party for him. All I know is he retired, at an age I consider fairly young. To be honest, I didn't even know he was still living around here."

I pulled out the photographs from a folder and handed them to Mike.

He said, "What's this?"

"The scene where Theresa Thompson had allegedly fallen down the stairs."

Mike gave me a look, like he was a bit suspicious. "How'd you get your hands on these? Paul?"

I shook my head.

Alex said, "It's probably best we don't say where we got them."

He stared back at Alex. "Didn't you hear what I—"

"Mike," she said, "It doesn't make a difference right now. Please, just listen."

I turned and stood shoulder to shoulder with Mike, pointing at the first photo on top, with Theresa's body at the bottom of the stairs. She was facedown, the way she had allegedly been found. "See the wineglass?" I said.

Mike looked the photo over, nodding. "Looks like it smashed under her when she fell."

"Does that make sense to you?" I said. "She tumbles down a full flight of stairs and doesn't drop her glass? Holding it in her hand until she falls on top of it?"

He studied the scene a little more without a response.

I flipped through the other photos. "Here, look. Now, do you see how the wine is all over the stairs? It's on the walls here"—I pointed—"and here. But if she kept it in front of her, there wouldn't be much of anything splashed on the wall. Not if she really grasped that glass."

Alex added, "It would've had to've been a pretty special glass to hold on to it, all the way down the stairs."

Mike said, "Please tell me you have something more than this."

I flipped to the next photo. "See how her glass is in her right hand? It's underneath her, but it's clearly her right hand."

"Yeah, so?"

I said, "We believe someone staged it to look like she took a tumble down the stairs after having one too many drinks."

Alex said, "Look at the next one."

I flipped to the close-up photos Alex had created on her computer. It was a zoomed-in image of the wine that had splashed on the wall and the drops on the stairs. "The wine is splashed on the left side. Her left side, coming down the stairs. Even the wine that had pooled on the steps is to her left."

"Are you trying to say she had the wine in her left hand?" Mike said. "But then why wasn't it on the left of her?" He shook his head. "The problem is, Walsh, that you can't tell me how she fell down those stairs. Not from these photos. She could've gone down backward before she turned, spinning... perhaps she tried to catch her fall."

I flipped to another close-up and pointed. "See the shape of these drops? She's going down, the wine comes out of the glass and splashes behind her. But you look at the shape of the wine drops. They splashed, and the way the wine hit the wall, you can tell it came from above, higher up the stairs."

Mike grabbed the photo from my hand and held it close to his face. He studied it some more, finally looking up from it. "There's no consistency to those markings."

I nodded. "Exactly. You look close enough, it's clear someone threw wine at the wall. It wouldn't look anything like this if the wine splashed from a glass as she's falling down the stairs."

He handed me the photos. "I understand where you're heading with this, but there's no way there's enough here to get a closed case reopened."

Alex said, "But don't you agree with Henry? It looks staged, once you look close enough."

Mike shrugged. "I'd have to study these photos a lot closer, but—"

"When Theresa Thompson died," I said, "John Thompson got a two-and-a-half-million-dollar settlement."

Mike said, "So you're going to try and say her husband killed her for the life insurance money? Don't you think the detective in charge at the time looked into that? It's Dead Spouse Investigations One-Oh-One."

Alex shook her head. "There was barely an investigation."

248

Mike took a drag from his cigarette. "The fact is, even if her husband killed her, what do you expect? They're both dead." He grinned, like he was proud of himself for the weak humor.

"I don't think John killed his wife," I said. "The one thing he did have, that's hard to dispute, was an alibi. People saw him coming home before he called the sheriff's office. Roy and a couple of men he was playing cards with all vouched for his whereabouts."

Mike removed his sunglasses, staring back at me. "Why do I get the feeling you're playing some kind of game with me?"

I said, "I'm not. But just because I don't think he killed her doesn't mean he wasn't involved. I still say whatever happened was covered up. And whoever did it, had help from someone over there at the sheriff's office."

Alex said, "No matter what actually happened, John got the full payout from her life insurance policy. But nobody ever knew he had it. And his stepson, who should've gotten a piece of it, got zero."

"Where was he during all this—the stepson?"

I could tell Mike was open to what we were saying, but I didn't think he appreciated the fact Alex and I were a few steps ahead of him.

I said, "Nate was at his aunt's house, who lives down in Gainesville. But here's the thing: I don't think John kept any of the money."

Mike held his gaze, waiting.

I said, "John owed Roy Mason two point five million, for a botched insurance claim. I have a feeling Roy got his money after Theresa was dead."

Mike looked away, toward the fountain. "Sounds to me you're making a pretty hefty assumption. Roy Mason knows a lot of people around here, and that includes within the sheriff's office. What evidence do you have that'll actually prove he had a hand in what might've happened?"

Alex held her gaze on Mike. "That's why we need your help."

Chapter 34

I DIDN'T RECOGNIZE THE number on my phone and cleared my throat to answer with my most professional voice. "Walsh Investigations."

"Henry? It's Lydia. I wasn't sure if I should call you or not, but I thought you should know that I'm on my way to meet Nate."

"Nate? You know where he is?"

I looked at Alex, stopped next to me, listening.

Lydia said, "Do you know where Thomas Creek Park is?"

"The conservation area?" I said.

"Yeah. That's where he is. He's hiding in an old hunting cabin, off one of the abandoned roads."

"Do you know why he called you?" I said. "Did he say anything else?"

"All he said was he needs my help."

I held the phone away from my ear and said to Alex, "Do you know how to get around Thomas Creek Park?"

She shrugged. "I know where it is."

I said into the phone, "What's the name of the road, the abandoned one?"

"It doesn't have a name, I don't think. But you just come in the east side of the park and look for it, about a half mile in on your right. You'll see it."

I thought for a moment. "Are you already there? You sound like you—"

"Nate gave me directions," she said. "That's how he described it."

Alex and I continued walking and climbed up into her Jeep.

Alex behind the wheel, she started the engine. "So we're heading northwest?"

I nodded to Alex and said to Lydia, "Does Nate know you called me?"

She was quiet for a few seconds. "Um, no. Not really."

I said, "What do you mean 'not really'? If you're not there yet, maybe you should wait for us. We're on our way." I looked at my watch. "Give us a half hour."

"He told me to hurry," she said.

"Just wait for me, all right?" I said. "At least wait out by the road. We'll be there soon."

"Okay, but if I'm not there, look for the trail on the right, from the east."

• • • • ● • ● • • •

Thomas Creek was east of Crawford, on the edge of Jacksonville. I called Lydia as soon as we'd passed the sign at the entrance, but her phone went right to voicemail. I didn't leave a message.

"Signal might be weak out here," Alex said, looking at her own phone.

I nodded, my eyes peeled for an abandoned road or trail on the right.

Alex drove fast along the main road from the entrance but started to slow down once we were about a mile in.

"You see anything?" I said, then spotted an opening in the woods with a rusted chain hung between two trees. "Stop!" I yelled, but Alex had already passed it, slamming on her brakes.

She turned the Jeep around and turned into the opening.

I jumped out and removed the chain attached to a hook on one of the trees, then waited for Alex to drive through. I reattached the chain on the hook and got back in the Jeep. "This has to be it."

The trees and thick vegetation was dense on either side of the road, overgrown branches hanging down toward the ground. Stick and rocks kicked up from the tires and pinged off the Jeep's undercarriage.

Alex tightened her grip on the steering wheel. "Why would he hide out here?"

"I'm still wondering why he's been hiding at all. If he was in some kind of trouble..."

"Maybe he doesn't trust you," Alex said. "Or anybody else."

At that point, we were deep into the woods. The path or road or whatever it was had become less visible, although it was clear from the tracks matting down the vegetation that another vehicle or two had come through ahead of us.

We turned a corner around the densely wooded area and stopped when an old, brown cabin came within view through the trees. It had a few small windows and a covered porch that stretched from one end of the cabin to the other. It looked like it might've been a nice place at one time, although it was clearly in disrepair.

Alex drove slowly and got us a little closer so we could get a better view. She stopped. "Where's Lydia's Jetta?"

Within the tall weeds and overgrown grass surrounding the cabin, was a set of vehicle tracks that continued around to the side.

I said, "Why would she park around the side?"

Alex turned off the engine. "Maybe those aren't her tracks."

We both stepped from the Jeep and started toward the cabin. Every few steps, we gave each other a glance, neither saying a word.

I went ahead of Alex when we got to the steps of the porch.

"What if this isn't the right place?" she said, walking through the tall grass and following the vehicle tracks. I watched as she pulled her Glock from her holster, disappearing around the corner toward the side.

I checked my phone, thinking I'd call Lydia to see if she was inside.

No signal.

The windows had curtains hanging, and I couldn't see inside. I stepped to the door, about to knock. It was quiet.

I waited a moment, then lifted my knuckles to rap on the door. But before I did, I heard a sound that'd quickly draw any man's attention.

A shotgun racked from behind me—sliding back, then forward.

I raised my hands, showing I was unarmed, and slowly turned around, looking into the double-barrel pointed at my chest.

On the other end of it was Roy Mason, the butt of the shotgun pressed inside his shoulder, one foot up on the bottom step.

Lydia was behind him, looking up at me from over his shoulder. "I'm sorry," she said, her voice hushed.

"She didn't do nothing but what I asked her to do," Roy said, giving me a nod with his chin. "Brian told me she thought she'd heard a conversation she shouldn't have—on the phone in the privacy of my own home—and once she understood what it was all about, she offered to do whatever I needed, to fix things." He again gave me a nod. "So here we are."

I eased my hands down to my sides, shifted my gaze from the double-barrel to the serious look on Roy's face. I said, "Are you trying to say you brought me here to make sure I get your so-called 'real' story? Or are you thinking maybe you'll pull that trigger, put and end to—"

"I'm not planning on killing you, to be honest. Just hoping you and I could have a word with each other, that's all."

I wondered if Roy was alone. He had to have known Alex was around the side, and I couldn't help but think something had already happened to her. "You didn't think to, maybe, I don't know, give me a phone call? Sit down for a few drinks instead of all this theater?"

Roy narrowed his eyes, cracking a smile. "Oh, it's not theater. I'll do what I gotta do. But I want to make sure you're doing the listening. That's all. I sincerely apologize if you feel I'm a bit over the top in my approach."

Under my breath, I said, "The apple doesn't fall far from the tree."

Roy put his hand up flat behind his ear, his palm toward me. "You got something you want to say?"

"I'm just saying, your son seems to take a similar approach. Can't help but think how the two of you always have something to hide."

"Nah, we're only protecting ourselves. That's all. You'd do the same thing, some stranger came around asking questions of you and your family... showing up in your place of business... at your home. For Brian, I'm all he's got." Roy looked over his shoulder at Lydia. "No offense, hon."

I said, "If you're trying to defend him—"

"He don't even know what he's protecting me from. He's just doing what he feels is right." Roy glanced toward the side of the house. "Why don't you tell your girlfriend to come on out before someone gets hurt." He raised an eyebrow. "She really thinks we didn't see her go round back?"

I stared back at Roy without saying a word.

He said, "I'm warning you right now, she'd be making a big mistake, she tries anything foolish."

Lydia had remained quiet, still hiding behind Roy, until he turned and handed her the twelve gauge and nodded toward the side of the cabin. "Make yourself useful, will you? Go find Ms. Jepson; tell 'er come on out front and say hello."

Roy pulled a long-barreled revolver from the waist of his pants and raised it toward me. "So I'm going to straighten some things out between us, tell you where things are at. You choose to believe me, maybe we both walk away from here with a better understanding of each other. If you decide you don't want to believe what I have to say, then perhaps you and I are gonna have ourselves a problem." Roy pointed with the revolver's barrel toward a grayed wooden picnic table that dipped down on one side, tall grass all around it. "Over there," he said, and waited for me to come down the steps and go ahead of him.

I walked toward the table, more worried about what Lydia would do with that twelve gauge if Alex happened to surprise her.

I sat on the bench, and the picnic table shifted, like it was going to flip.

Roy came over, his gun pointed toward me, and put one foot up on the other side of the table, keeping it from lifting.

At that point, he rested his revolver on his knee. "You need to understand, first and foremost, that I did not kill John." He looked toward the Jeep, a good thirty feet away, before shifting his gaze back to me. "God's honest truth is what that is."

"Then why were you at his house, before anyone else had even found him, like you already knew something nobody else did?"

Roy laughed. "I was there when the officers first showed up at her door. That was the first moment I'd learned of his passing."

"His *passing*?"

Roy gave a quick nod.

"But why were you there? You knew John was out on his bike, as he'd been every single Sunday morning."

"I dropped off John's golf clubs. He'd left them in my trunk from the week before, but I knew he'd been away those few days."

"With Kayla," I said.

Roy stared back at me, eyebrows raised.

I said, "The fact he was screwing around with her, aside, why don't you tell me why I should believe you had nothing to do with his death?"

"It's the truth, son."

I looked toward the corner of the house, where Alex had gone.

"She doesn't do anything foolish," Roy said, glancing in the same direction I was, "she'll be all right."

I could have called for Alex, but I didn't. I had a feeling she was up to something, and clearly Lydia hadn't found her.

"Okay, so you didn't kill him. But then why don't you go ahead and try to explain to me what happened to the money John got after Theresa died? It seems to me your relationship with John must've healed quite well once Theresa was dead, and John had all that money. What a coincidence, huh? Just happens to be the amount you felt John owed you for the mistake he made on your policy."

"You know what?" Roy said. "I'm not going to deny all that. The truth is, John owed me a lot of money. What happened with that, uh, unfortunate mistake on my coverage caused some real friction between him and me. Just because he was able to cover his mistake due to an unfortunate accident, doesn't mean—"

"You're seriously going to call what happened to her an accident, too?" I said. "Like you and your friends at the sheriff's office have done with John?"

"Come again?" Roy said.

"You heard me," I said. "You expect me to believe her death was an accident?" I said. "She dies, and it's just a coincidence John receives a payout from her life insurance that happens to cover what he owed you for such a costly mistake?"

"So, now you're not only accusing me of killing my good friend, but his wife?" He shook his head. "Maybe this won't be as easy as I'd hoped it'd be."

259

Alex turned the corner, Lydia walking behind her with the twelve gauge pointed at her back.

Roy said, "You take it easy there, Lydia. You can put that thing down for now." He waved for Alex. "Why don't you come join us? We're just having a friendly conversation."

Alex walked over and stood next to me.

I wished I could tell her everything would be fine. I turned back to Roy. "I know Theresa's death, like John's, was more than just an accident. We have the proof we need to show the whole scene was staged. And if you'd like to think killing us means that proof'll disappear... I hate to say it, but you'd be wrong."

The picnic table shifted when Roy straightened up and took his foot off the bench. He tucked the revolver in his pants and looked toward the woods. "I used to hunt out here with my daddy, you know."

Roy appeared calm and a little too relaxed.

"Roy," I said. "Why don't you admit you helped John kill Theresa so he could get you the money you felt he owed you?"

Roy slowly turned toward me. "John Thompson wouldn't hurt a fly. He had his faults, like the rest of us. I'd say number one was, he liked the ladies a little too much. Could barely control himself, think straight. The man couldn't help but fall in love with any woman who breathed his way. But"—Roy shook his head—"he didn't kill Theresa. And that money he gave me? I never asked him for it. There was no big plan, if that's what you're thinking. That's the truth. In fact, I knew nothing about what'd happened. Not until later. But John used an opportunity to make a wrong right again. And I wasn't going to argue with him, either."

I said, "Did you even know that it wasn't John that made the mistake on your policy? Did you know it was his brother, who John wanted to protect?"

Roy nodded. "Eric told me some time ago. John, of course, never said a word. That's the kind of man he was. It didn't matter John didn't like his brother very much; he still took the blame. Mainly, because it was his company. John was an honorable man, in some ways. And he would never throw someone in his own family under the bus."

"But he'd throw his wife down the stairs?" I said.

Roy shook his head. "That's just not the truth. I don't know how else to tell you that."

We all stood, quiet. I didn't know how we were going to get out of it, other than hoping Roy meant what he said about not wanting to kill us.

"So what do we do from here?" I said.

Roy took a moment before he answered. "Do you believe what I'm telling you?"

I had to think about it. "I guess, right now, I don't have much of a choice but to tell you I do."

"That doesn't sound very sincere," he said.

"I have no proof you had anything to do with what happened to Theresa. And there's no evidence to indicate you killed John. But the fact remains, somebody did."

Chapter 35

To say I was surprised Roy let us leave without incident would be an understatement. My gut told me not to trust him, and I couldn't help but question his honesty. But nonetheless, Alex and I were back out on the road, headed toward 295, wondering where to go from there, if we were to believe Roy's story.

Alex's phone rang. "It's Mike." She answered on the next ring. "Mike?" She listened, nodding with the phone up to her ear. "He's actually right here," she said, without mentioning what had happened on the edge of Thomas Creek Park. "Actually, I'm in the car with Henry. He should hear this, if it's okay I put you on speaker?" She pulled off the highway and into the breakdown lane, resting the phone on the center console between us. "Okay, Mike, go ahead."

"As I was telling you, I went through all available customer records at Paul Krueger's gym. With the help of some of the staff, we were able to match one of the names to the white truck. The man's name is Ronald Phillips, although we haven't yet been able to track down a registration under that name. According to the owner of the gym, the front of the truck had the black bull bar."

I said, "Ronald Phillips? Is he from around here?"

"As of right now, we have a match of someone who's originally from St. Augustine, but had a recent address out in Jacksonville Beach. Officers checked into it, but there's no such person living in the apartment complex. The manager said it'd been about two months since Phillips moved out, never paid a dime in rent."

Alex leaned toward the phone. "Is there any other obvious connection to Brian Mason?"

"Nothing beyond the fact they used to work out at the same gym. Owner I spoke with confirmed what he'd told you. This guy didn't appear to be a friend of Mason's. He's also got a rap sheet with a couple of sexual assaults on it, a half-dozen B & E's when he was younger, and—this one'll hit home—attempted murder. None led to any convictions."

The phone went quiet, me and Alex looking at each other.

Alex said, "Mike? Are you still there?"

"Yeah, I'm here. But that's all I've got, so far. Just thought you'd like to know. Oh, and there's still nothing yet on Nate Ryan's whereabouts."

I said, "What about Theresa Thompson's case?"

"If you're asking if I figured out who might've clamped down and held up the investigation, I don't know. I'm working on it. I can't just go around headquarters, asking who's a crooked cop."

I said, "It's got to be someone who was close enough to Sergeant Meredith at the time. He's the one who pushed him to get Paul Krueger out of there."

"You don't think I know that?" Mike said. "You'd better hold your horses. I'm already putting my neck on the line here. And, Walsh, I think if anyone knows what happens when you try to turn against a fellow officer, it's you."

Mike loved to bring up my past, twisting the knife when he had the chance.

I said, "You're not turning against anyone, Mike. We're all after the same thing here. Remember?"

"Don't get preachy with me. Okay? I'll let you know when I have something more. You're welcome."

Alex picked up the phone and looked at the screen. "He hung up."

• • • • • • • • • •

Alex was anxious to check on Raz. He'd made himself right at home upstairs at Billy's Place, and I wondered if she was afraid he might never want to leave. Especially with Billy giving Raz leftover steak at the end of each night.

I was already at the bar when Alex came down with him, had him sit down next to her at the foot of her stool. She pulled her laptop from her bag.

Billy leaned with his hands on the bar and kept asking questions about our crazy run-in with Roy. "Just so I have this straight. He holds you at gunpoint, so you'd listen to him? And he explains how he ended up with the two and a half million, but didn't admit he knew it had anything to do with the death of John's wife?"

I said, "He knows he looks guilty as hell, so I guess he figured he had to go to extremes to make sure I got his side of the story."

Billy seemed surprised. "So you told him you believed him, and he let you go?"

"With a gun pointed at my face, I tend to become somewhat agreeable."

Billy said to Alex, "What'd your cop friend have to say about it?"

Alex looked up from her laptop. "Who, Mike?"

"No, the other one. The good-looking one you were here with the other night? I thought you said he was helping you out?"

"Oh, Chris? He got us some photos, but for the most part, he thinks it's best he stay out of it. Especially now that Mike's agreed to help."

Billy poured himself a coffee and took a sip, resting the cup on the bar. "So, this guy Chris... was he an old boyfriend?"

Alex hesitated for a moment, then shook her head. "No, we went to the academy together, up in Virginia."

"Ohhh," Billy said. "I thought he was, well, I guess I figured maybe he was an old fling."

She gave Billy a dirty look. "Not at all."

"Oh, sorry. I thought..." Billy turned and walked over to the window from the kitchen, grabbed two plates of food and carried them over to us. "Here's something to eat," he said. "Let me know if you need anything else."

I shoved a couple of fries in my mouth as if I hadn't eaten in days.

Alex turned her laptop so I could see the screen, where she'd put together a diagram of everyone who, at one point or another, we'd either spoken with, or who had some kind of dealings with John—both business and personal. Each picture had a name typed under it. She said, "I'm still going through all the names, but so far every person here is born and raised right here in Jax."

"All of them?" I said.

"I'm not done yet." She pulled the laptop toward her again. "What's Michelle Thompson's maiden name?"

"Heathwood." I took a bite of the sandwich and nodded toward the plate Billy had put in front of Alex. "I thought you were hungry? You haven't touched a thing."

Without taking her eyes from the screen, she continued typing. "You go right ahead and stuff your face. I'll take care of solving the crimes."

I laughed, taking another bite. "I don't remember the last time I ate!"

She reached for my plate, took a french fry and stuck it in her mouth. Then she wiped her hands on a napkin and started typing again. She said, "Here it is. Ronald Phillips. He graduated from St. Augustine High, seventeen years ago."

I looked at her screen, wiping my mouth. "So that makes him, what, around thirty-four?" I pushed my plate aside and stood up, looking over Alex's shoulder so I could get a better view.

Billy stepped over, leaning on the bar. "Find something?"

I nodded. "Could be the man who tried to kill us."

"And Kayla Morton," Alex said.

Billy said, "Do you have a picture of him?"

Alex swung the laptop toward him, and he slipped his reading glasses on, looking at the screen.

Billy's eyes widened, looking from me to Alex. "He looks familiar. I don't know why. Maybe he's been here?" He was quiet, pulling at his chin. He slapped the bar. "That's it!" Billy looked toward the door. "He was here the other night." Billy scanned the tables along the bar.

"He was *here*?" I said. "Are you sure?"

Billy nodded. "He was in here the same night that kid came looking for you."

"Nate?"

"Yes. I didn't think anything of it, but now I remember. I saw them glance at each other, almost like they were up to something. And I'm pretty sure he left right after that kid, Nate."

Chapter 36

I STOOD OUTSIDE IN the back parking lot of the dentist's office, where the late Sgt. Andy Meredith's widow, Marie, worked as a dental hygienist.

She walked out the back door from the building and across the parking lot, with barely enough space to fit the six cars already parked there.

"Marie?" I said, walking toward her.

She, at first, appeared somewhat startled, reaching her hand into the purse hung from her shoulder.

I put my hands up. "I don't know what you're about to pull out of your purse, but before you do... my name is Henry Walsh. I'm a private investigator here in Jax. I want to ask you a few questions about your husband."

She didn't seem to care *who* I was. Her hand came out from her purse with a small Ruger revolver in her grasp.

I kept my hands in the air, extending my index finger. "Please, just one minute to explain."

"What have you done with my husband?" She pointed the gun at me. "Where is he?"

"Your husband? Isn't he dead?"

She cocked her head. "Leon?"

"Who's Leon?"

"My husband."

"Oh, I'm sorry. But aren't you Andy Meredith's widow?"

She breathed out a sigh. "Oh, I thought..." She smiled. "I'm remarried now. As of six weeks ago."

I said, "Okay, so you're not Mrs. Meredith anymore?"

"Mrs. Connor."

I nodded toward the Ruger in her hand, my hands lowered but still up where she could see them. "Would you mind putting that thing away?"

"Do you have any ID? What did you say you were—a PI?"

I nodded, pulling a card from my pocket.

She grabbed it from my hand and looked it over before handing it back to me.

"You can keep the card," I said. "I have a whole box of them."

Marie stuck the card in her purse, her other hand still holding the pistol but it was down by her side. "You look harmless. But I've made that mistake in judgment before." She slipped the Ruger back in her purse and slid the zipper across the top.

I eased my hands down. "Is it okay for us to talk here?"

She turned and looked at the door to her building, shaking her head. "There's already enough gossip behind that door. I'd rather go somewhere else. There's a restaurant down the street, a Chinese place. Food's not great, but the drinks are cheap. And we can talk without anybody listening."

• • • ● • ● • • •

Marie was already seated at the bar with a drink in her hand when I walked into Wa Ma Wok's. If it weren't for the instrumental eighties' music coming from the speakers, I would've assumed the place was closed.

I said, "Is there a bartender? Or is it self-serve?"

Marie smiled and stood up from her stool, leaning on the bar. "Liena? Are you back there, hon? You've got a customer."

A young woman stepped through red curtains hanging across a doorway behind the bar, and wiped her hands on her apron. She smiled at me. "Hello."

Marie said, "Liena, my new friend would like a drink."

She smiled again, nodding. "What would you like?"

I thought about having a whiskey but decided against it. "I'll have a bottle of Budweiser."

The young woman reached into the glass-doored refrigerator and grabbed a bottle of Bud, placing it on the bar with a small glass.

"Thank you," I said, pushing the glass back toward her. "The bottle's fine."

She stood and watched me take a sip, then disappeared through the curtained doorway without another word.

"She's the owner's sister," Marie said. "Nice kid, but she's lucky there's never more than two or three people ordering drinks." She smiled, turning to face me, leaning with her elbow on the bar. "So, why don't you go ahead and tell me what this is all about?"

I said, "I was hired to investigate John Thompson's death."

She was about to take a drink but stopped, placing the glass back down. "John Thompson?" She straightened in her seat, looking straight ahead. "If I'd known this had something to do with—"

"I guess I don't need to tell you who he is?"

She took a moment without answering, then slowly turned to me. "Of course I do. He used to say he was a friend of my late husband's."

I said, "By your tone, I'm guessing that wasn't the case?"

Marie folded her arms on the bar, looking into her drink. "John was the kind of friend who only came around when he needed something." She turned a little more my way. "They played ball together in high school. John left for college, and I don't think Andy heard from him again until..." She cleared her throat. "What do you want?"

I watched her, like she was hesitant to make eye contact. "I'm guessing you know who Paul Krueger is?"

She finally faced me. "Why?"

"Well, first of all, he spoke very highly of your husband. But Krueger also said it was your husband who forced him into retirement from the sheriff's office. He believed he was forced to resign soon after he reported to the scene of Theresa Thompson's death."

"I haven't heard his name in quite some time," Marie said. "But"—she looked at me—"what do you expect me to say? That my husband was wrong to force Paul out? That he was up to no good? That I know all the secrets?" She reached for her wine, shaking her head. "I'm sorry, but—"

"I need to understand what happened."

Marie picked up her glass and sipped her wine. "Why are you assuming I'd know anything about it?"

"Because he was your husband," I said. "I'm asking you to tell me what you know."

"Why should I?"

I swallowed and sipped my drink. "Because I don't believe Theresa's death was an accident. And your husband may have been killed because he knew the truth."

She appeared to be getting upset, the way she bit at her lower lip. "If I tell you what I know, can you promise me I won't be pulled into something I've worked hard to put behind me?" She stared at me. "This conversation will stay between us, okay? I've spent the last five years of my life trying to block it all out. I've started over. And the last thing I need is—"

"I'll do what I can to make sure you're not dragged into it."

She shook her head. "No. That's not good enough. It's a simple yes-or-no answer. You have to promise you'll keep me out of it. I want nothing to do with the legal process. I don't want to be a witness or pulled into some damn trial."

I nodded, although I wasn't sure I was the one to make her the promise she was looking for.

She called out for Liena, and the young woman came through the curtain. "Can I help you, Miss Marie?"

Marie pushed her empty glass across the bar. "More wine, please."

Liena nodded with a big smile and filled Marie's glass, almost to the top, then smiled as she asked me, "Would you like another beer, sir?"

I'd hardly touched it. "I'm good for now, thanks."

Liena nodded and again disappeared through the curtain.

Marie took a good sip from her glass, pausing a moment with her elbow down, her chin rested in her hand. "The night Theresa Thompson was found dead..." She paused, looking toward the doorway with the curtain. She kept her voice quiet, almost in a whisper. "John showed up at our door. I don't remember what time it was, but Andy and I were in bed. Maybe it was midnight, or a little later. Andy jumped from bed when he heard the knock—we were both startled—and got up, answering the door. I followed him and stood behind him from inside, watching John. The man was shaking, standing out on the porch. He was a mess. It seemed like he'd been drinking, but I don't know that for sure. It was hard to see out there." She took a moment, with an expression like she was thinking. "I can still see the dim bulb in the lamp over the door, shining on his face."

"What did he say to your husband?"

"That he needed Andy's help. Something bad had happened."

"Did he say what it was?" I said.

Marie shook her head. "Andy told me to go back to bed, stepped out onto the porch with John and closed the door behind him."

"You didn't hear anything?"

She waited before responding, then nodded. "I listened, as much as I could. John wasn't being quiet. He bordered on being hysterical, the way he sounded. I knew it was something about Theresa, but I didn't know why until I heard him say she was dead. When the door opened, and Andy walked in, he saw me standing there but didn't explain what it was about. I didn't ask. All he said was he had to go help John.

Andy went to the bedroom and got dressed, headed out the door without another word.

"He left with John?"

She shook her head. "He'd never driven my car before, but he took it that night."

I said, "He didn't tell you anything?"

"No. He came home an hour, maybe an hour and a half later... got back in bed without saying a word. Next day I heard about Theresa's death, and remembered seeing Paul Krueger on TV. They showed him outside the Thompsons' home. I remember turning from the TV, looking at Andy, just sitting there at the kitchen table. He was in uniform, sipping his coffee without saying two words. He wouldn't look at me, and I knew right then..."

I said, "Even in the morning? He wouldn't tell you what happened?"

"Not then. But it was less than a week later, I knew Paul was no longer with the sheriff's office. He'd retired. But I didn't believe it; it made no sense." She took a deep breath, eyes closed for a brief moment. "I had no choice, and confronted Andy."

"Did he tell you... did he tell you John Thompson killed his wife?"

She hesitated, picked up her glass, shaking her head, and said, "John didn't kill his wife."

Chapter 37

ALEX WAS SEATED WITH her laptop at one of the high-top tables at Billy's Place, papers spread out in front of her. I gave Billy a nod behind the bar and sat across from Alex. "I met with Marie Connor."

"Marie Connor?" Alex said. "Who's that?"

"Andy Meredith's widow. She got remarried a month and a half ago."

Billy walked around the bar and came over to sit with us, pulling up a chair between me and Alex. "Any news?"

I nodded. "I was telling Alex that I met with Andy Meredith's wife. I didn't know this, but she said John and her late husband were friends in high school. They played baseball together."

"I assume there's more?" Alex said, raising her eyes from her laptop.

Billy folded his arms, pulling at his chin. "Tell me again who Andy Meredith is?"

"He's the sergeant who forced Paul Krueger into retirement."

"And Paul's the one who investigated Theresa Thompson's death?"

"Sort of. He was never officially allowed to, beyond that very first night he took the call. And he was off the force a week later."

Billy had a surprised look on his face. "Sounds familiar, doesn't it?"

"That's what I told Krueger. Maybe we get done with this whole thing, I'll take him for a beer so we can swap stories." I turned to Alex and said, "Marie told me John showed up at their door in the middle of the night, asking Andy for his help."

Alex leaned toward me. "The night of Theresa's death?"

I nodded, and continued telling them everything Marie had told me, and where it left us. "We should talk to Mike," I said.

"I just got off the phone with him, about twenty minutes ago. One thing he mentioned was a young officer who ended up in the ER after suffering an allergic reaction. His whole body was covered in blisters, on top of respiratory issues, because it somehow got into his lungs."

Billy said, "From *what*?"

"Poison sumac. Rookie cop, had no idea he was highly allergic."

I thought for a moment. "What's it look like?"

Alex shrugged. "Poison sumac?" She typed the keys on her laptop, then showed me a photo of someone's upper body, covered in blisters.

"That's disgusting," I said. "But I hope the kid's all right?"

Billy said, "Can someone tell me what you're talking about?"

Alex said to him, "One of the officers on the scene at Losco Park—where John Thompson was killed—reached into the shrubs to retrieve John's helmet. Kid breaks out a couple of hours later, ends up having an allergic reaction to what turned out to be poison sumac."

Billy scratched his arm. "Makes me itchy just thinking about it. I had no idea poison sumac was that bad. I used to get poison ivy when I was a kid, but it doesn't bother me anymore."

I said, "And what about the kid at the record store? They get anything else from him?"

"Like I told you on the phone, he never saw who shot him. It happened so fast."

"So he doesn't think Nate could've been involved?"

"Wait," Billy said. "You think Nate could've shot the kid at the record store?"

"There's a theory that he might've set it all up to make it look like he was abducted. But it's just something getting tossed around."

"Yeah?" Billy said.

Alex nodded. "And the kid—the one who got shot—thinks he saw a white pickup out back earlier in the day, but can't confirm."

"The white pickup truck? The one that almost killed you?"

I said to Billy, "There's a chance he's a friend of Nate's."

Billy stared back at me but didn't seem to be following.

Alex typed on her laptop. "Take a look at this."

I pulled it closer, looking at the photo Alex had pulled up. "Is that..."

"Same graduating class," she said. "They dated for three years. I spoke with the school secretary, an older woman who'd been there for the past thirty years. She remembers them both."

"Who?" Billy said, still trying to keep up with the long threads we were trying to tie together.

"Ron Phillips. He's the owner of the white Ford truck."

Alex said, "The woman I spoke with, from the school, said he was in and out of trouble as a kid. She also said she never understood what she saw in him."

"What *who* saw in him?" Billy said, scratching his head, looking at us both. "Will someone tell me what's going on?"

I took out my phone and showed Billy a picture of John and Michelle Thompson together. I spun the laptop toward him so he could see the picture on the screen.

"See the young girl in the photo on Alex's computer?"

Billy squinted, nodding. "Good-looking kid."

"Now look at the picture of Michelle Thompson."

279

Billy got up and grabbed his reading glasses from the bar. He sat back down and took my phone, then looked at Alex's laptop. "That's her? Michelle Thompson? And who's this guy?"

"Ronnie Thompson," I said.

Billy's eyes opened wide, looking from me to Alex. "Were they—"

"High school sweethearts," Alex said.

Chapter 38

I STOOD OUTSIDE THE front door of Michelle Thompson's house after ringing the bell for a third time. When she finally came to the door, she appeared out of sorts, covering what I felt was a look of surprise, behind a smile that was a little too forced. She pushed open the glass storm door and leaned out, looking past me, toward the street.

"Henry," she said. "Mickey let you in?"

"Took some convincing," I said. "Especially after you'd told him not to."

She pushed out an unconvincing smile. "Me? Is that what he said?" She laughed, brushing it off with the sweep of her hand. "Mickey doesn't always hear things the right way."

"Mickey's smarter than you think," I said.

She pushed her hair back from her forehead, the smile beginning to weaken.

"Mind if I come inside?" I didn't wait for her answer and pushed my way past her. The sweet smell of cookies hung in the air. "You're baking more cookies?"

Michelle followed me down the hall toward her kitchen. "I... I'm on my way out," she said. "I have an appointment. I'm sorry, but you're going to have to leave."

"This won't take long," I said. "At least, I don't think it will. But you still may want to tell whoever it is you're meeting that you might not be able to make it." She stepped past me, walking to the stove.

She pulled a pan of cookies from the oven and placed them on a heating pad on the counter.

"So," I said. "Where is he?" I hadn't moved from the doorway.

Michelle turned. "I'm sorry? Where is *who*?"

"Nate." I looked behind me, down the hall toward the open front door.

There was what looked like a silver metal tray with cookies stacked on it, placed on the counter between me and Michelle.

She stood still, her mouth open as if she were about to say something but didn't.

I watched her eyes look toward the hallway, and when I turned, Nate was there, just a few feet away.

He had a gun in his grasp, and he raised it, pointing it straight at me.

I didn't want to take my eyes off Nate, but I didn't trust Michelle, either. She hadn't moved from the other side of the counter. I said to Nate, "Is that the same gun you used to shoot your friend at the record store?"

Nate shook his head. "He's not really much of a friend."

"But you shot him," I said. "For *what*? So you could set it up so you could disappear, then come over here and snuggle up with your nanny?"

Nate squinted his eyes, full of anger, holding the gun in front of him with both hands.

I said to Michelle, "I gotta be honest. When I thought maybe it was Roy you were sleeping with, I knew he was a little too old for you. But now, this is just as weird. The nanny? I mean"—I looked at Nate, then back at Michelle—"throw in the fact you're married to his stepfather and—"

"Don't call him that," Nate said, the anger clear in his voice.

"So why didn't you shoot him?" I said. "Use that gun you have right there in your hands. Instead of going through all the trouble to set up a foolish bike accident." He still had the red bumps on his arm. "Looks like the poison sumac hasn't completely cleared up? That stuff can be nasty, you know."

Nate looked at his arms, with the gun still in his grasp and pointed my way.

Michelle said, "Nate, don't say a word. He has no idea what he's talking about." She moved from behind the counter to where she could see Nate, but was still behind it.

I watched her look toward a wooden block of knives and wondered why I always showed up unarmed. But that decision had already been made. I glanced at the tray of cookies.

"So, why'd you do it, Nate? For love? Or because you think John killed your mother?"

"He *did* kill my mother!" he yelled.

I saw a different side of Nate he'd obviously suppressed quite well until that point.

I turned to Michelle. "At least someone believes you."

She kept her eyes on me as I turned to Nate, staring back at Michelle.

"He knows the truth," Michelle said. "He knows John killed his mother. And then kept all her life insurance money to himself. Nate deserved better than that." She smiled at Nate. "Right, hon?"

I said, "Okay. Well then, if that's the way you're going to tell the story... I assume you helped him kill John?" I turned to Nate. "And I'm guessing she'll share something with you, from John's insurance?"

Nate didn't answer. He looked nervous, holding the gun like he didn't know what to do with it.

That didn't make me too comfortable, to be honest.

"Nate, just to set the record straight," I said. "I know you want to believe what Michelle has told you. But John did *not* kill your mother. Now, did he give you the shaft by not giving you the insurance money from your mother's policy?" I nodded. "Of course he did. But he did *not* kill her. His only crime was trying to cover up what really happened." I looked at Michelle. "He was only guilty of trying to protect the woman he loved."

Nate stepped closer to me but only so he could get a better look at Michelle. "Michelle? What is he talking about?"

She shook her head. "Don't listen to him, Nate. He has no idea what he's saying."

"No?" I watched Michelle take a step away from us, and it looked like she was heading toward the block of knives. I said, "Nate, do you really want to be a private investigator?"

Nate shook his head. "No, not really."

"I didn't think so," I said, keeping my eye on Michelle. "Now, Nate... why don't you put down the gun, okay?" I tried to watch them both, unsure who was going to make the first move.

Michelle leaned over the counter, looking at him. "You have to shoot him, Nate. Do you understand? You have no choice."

Nate stared back at her, the gun tight in his grasp.

I held my hands up, palms toward him. "Nate, don't. I can help you. Just hear me out..."

"Shoot him!" Michelle screamed.

"Nate, there were plenty of witnesses that night. John had an alibi. And not just his friends. There was even footage of him stopping at a 7-Eleven, and she'd already been dead when he'd stopped."

Michelle yelled. "Nate! Listen to me. John killed your mother. I saw the whole thing."

Out of the corner of my eye, I saw Michelle reach for a chef's knife and pull it from the wooden block. She came around the counter and lunged at me with the knife.

I reached for the silver tray of cookies on the counter and swung it, along with at least a dozen cookies, striking Michelle's arm. The knife came free as the tray hit her, spinning in the air toward me. The blade nicked the back of my hand and hit the floor.

Nate came at me with the gun raised, eyes closed with his finger on the trigger, as if he was about to pull it.

I still had the cookie tray in my hand and swung it again, this time knocking the gun from Nate's hand.

A shot fired as it fell from his grasp.

Michelle screamed, stumbling backward, trying to grab the edge of the counter as she fell to the floor, whimpering.

Nate tried to reach for the gun, but I grabbed him by his shirt and threw him against the wall, cracking his head against a framed photo of John and Michelle that smashed when it hit the floor.

I tossed Nate out of my way and I hurried over to where Michelle lay.

She held her hand on her shoulder, blood coming through her fingers. "He shot me," she cried.

I knew he didn't mean to shoot her, but I didn't bother telling her.

I jumped to my feet when Nate got up and came around the counter. I had expected him to attack me, but he didn't.

He stood, looking down at Michelle and the puddle of blood on the floor. A tear came down his cheek, and he looked like a scared little boy. He said, "Is she going to die?"

Chapter 39

NATE SAT QUIETLY IN the back seat of the cruiser parked in the middle of the driveway. With his wrists handcuffed behind his back, he stared straight ahead toward Michelle and John Thompson's house.

Mike Stone walked over to me and Alex, standing outside the cruiser with Nate inside it. "You'll be happy to hear the police've found a white F-250 down in Gainesville, parked outside a gym. Ronald Phillips is inside, but police, along with a handful of U.S. Marshals, are about to make an arrest. It's only a matter of time." He turned toward the rescue parked in front of the garage. "Bullet only grazed her shoulder."

"So I guess she'll live?" Alex said.

Mike nodded, then leaned and glanced in through the window at Nate in the back seat. He said, "Does he know his nanny's the one who killed his mother?" He straightened himself from the window and looked me in the eye.

"Not yet," I said. "Won't do much good at this point. Maybe something his lawyer will be able to use."

"I'm not sure a judge out there'll give him much leniency. Twenty-two-year-old kid kills his stepfather, sets it up to look like a bike accident. Not to mention having a romantic relationship with the victim's wife." Mike shook his head. "Of course, it was clearly premeditated." He held up the digital recorder I'd had in my pocket when I was inside with Nate and Michelle. "Looks like you got us what we need."

Alex said, "I still find it hard to believe Paul Krueger kept his mouth shut all these years."

"Who knows," Mike said. "Have to wonder if maybe Mr. Thompson gave him a little something, to keep him quiet."

"You think so?" I said.

Mike said, "Can't think of any other reason he'd keep quiet. Especially when he lost his job over it." He walked away without saying much else, heading toward the EMS vehicle. He stopped and turned, giving me and Alex a nod. "The sheriff's office appreciates the cooperation."

Alex smiled.

I looked up at the big house John and Michelle Thompson had lived in together. "You see these people, all the money in the world. I mean, at least that's what they'd like everyone to think. The big house, the expensive cars... while everything else crumbles around them."

"You say it like this was all about the money," Alex said.

"It all grows from the same seed," I said, looking at Mike up near the side of the garage, smoking a cigarette. "Hey, Mike."

He turned, and I pointed toward the cruiser with Nate in the back. "Mind if I have a few words with Nate?"

Mike stared back for a moment before answering, took a drag of his cigarette, and gave me a nod.

I reached for the back door on the driver's side and ducked inside. Nate wouldn't turn or look at me, his gaze going the other way out the window.

"Nate, there's something you need to know," I said.

After a moment, he faced me. "Is she okay?"

I nodded. "Yeah, she's fine. You barely got her. Couple of stitches'll take care of it. But they're taking her in, get her checked out to make sure."

"There was a lot of blood," he said, a shake to his voice. He had the look of a little boy, a scared little boy, and not the man—the killer—he actually was.

I said, "She'll be fine."

He turned again and looked out the window to his right.

"Nate, you need to know who really killed your mother."

Without looking at me, he said, "I know who did it."

"Do you understand what that means?"

His eyes met mine for a moment. "I killed John because I thought he killed my mom. I never thought in a million years Michelle could do such a thing. I..." He paused. "I really thought she loved me as much as I loved her."

I looked through the front windshield as the med techs pushed Michelle up into the back of the EMS vehicle. Mike watched her from a few feet away, the cigarette in his mouth.

Nate said, "But why'd she lie to me? Why not stick with the story that it was an accident. Why'd she tell me John killed my mom? Just so I'd help her get him out of her life?" Nate shook his head. "She was always so manipulative."

I said, "Are you telling me it had nothing to do with the life insurance?"

"My mom's?"

"Well, no. That's gone. I'm talking about John's policy. Wasn't Michelle going to give you a cut from John's life insurance? To make up for the money you never received from your mother's?"

Nate appeared to hesitate but then decided to come clean. "We were supposed to split it three ways."

I said, "Ronald Phillips?"

Nate stared straight ahead, nodding.

"What I don't understand," I said, "is why did you tell me you saw Ronald's truck at Kayla's?"

Nate was quiet for a moment. "I wanted him out of the way. I thought—"

"You thought you could maybe pin it on him, and you and Michelle could be together?"

Again, Nate didn't answer.

An officer came up to the car, opened the door and leaned in. "Time to go."

290

I started to rise from the seat but glanced back at Nate for a moment before I got out.

Alex stood behind the officer. "Michelle threw the old boyfriend under the bus, said Ron Phillips killed Kayla."

Chapter 40

ALEX AND I SAT out on the dock near my boat, watching the sun set on the backside of the St. Johns.

A dark BMW pulled up into the space next to the old Chevy Chevelle I'd picked up from Billy's house a few hours earlier. Angela stepped out from the car, a bottle in one hand and a white envelope in the other.

Raz lifted his head, and the three of us watched her walk toward the dock. I stood and took a lawn chair from the boat and unfolded it, placing it next to mine.

Angela handed me a bottle of Jack Daniels and the white envelope, then looked at the aluminum lawn chair with the green-vinyl webbing. "I included a little bonus in there for you. Maybe get yourself some new lawn furniture." She stared out toward the water. "Or *dock* furniture... whatever you call it."

"I appreciate the gesture. But I'll replace these only once they no longer hold me off the ground." I pointed at the chair. "Have a seat. They're comfortable."

Angela smiled. "I didn't know they still made these chairs. It's all they had when we were kids."

I didn't tell her they were my family's chairs from when I was a kid.

"Can I get you a glass of wine?" I said.

Angela shook her head. "I was hoping you'd pour us all a glass of whiskey."

I stepped toward the boat, but Alex grabbed me by the arm. "Sit down. I'll get some glasses."

Alex went up on the boat, with Raz behind her.

"I have to be honest," Angela said. "I'm still surprised." She paused. "*Shocked* might be a better word." She folded one leg over the other. "There was a point there, as you know, when I had my doubts. Not just about you, but I thought maybe I'd been wrong the whole time." She looked me in the eye. "I want to apologize for that."

I said, "Maybe that's why you and I got along. It's like, you don't always know what you're looking for, but you know something's there. And you won't give up until you find it."

Angela leaned toward me. "You know, if I didn't know Alex had such a strong hold on your heart, maybe you and I—"

"Alex?" I shook my head. "We're friends."

Angela laughed. "Go right on fooling yourselves, okay? You just got through saying 'you know something's there,' but—"

Alex stepped down off the boat and onto the dock, handing a glass to me and Angela and poured us each a shot.

"You're not having any?" Angela said.

293

Alex shook her head. "Not right now."

Angela raised her glass. "Here's to the two of you. Best detectives in Florida." She took a sip and made a face like someone who hadn't had whiskey before.

Alex's phone buzzed, and she pulled it from her pocket, looking at the screen. "Good news: Ron Phillips is in custody." She patted Raz's head.

Angela said, "Can you explain to me where this man came from?"

I threw back my shot of Jack and filled my glass with another. "Michelle had been sleeping with him. For quite a while, in fact. I guess she went back home and—"

"Home? To where? St. Augustine?"

I nodded. "He'd moved up this way—actually out at Jacksonville Beach."

Alex said, "Far enough away... but close enough they could get together."

I said, "But he left the apartment right after John was killed."

"And she convinced him to kill John?" Angela said.

I shook my head. "I think it was both of them. When Nate started coming around, they had to change their plans, pulling Nate in to help do the job. And once you hired me, their only focus was getting rid of me. And Alex."

Angela said, "Sounds like Nate must've built up a lot of hate for John."

"And Michelle simply fed the fire by convincing him John killed Theresa," I said. "But all John was guilty of was covering it up to protect Michelle... the woman who plotted to kill him."

The three of us stood, quiet.

I said, "Michelle is still saying the whole thing was an accident."

Angela said, "You mean Theresa's death?"

"She said she was there waiting for John to come home. She'd sent Nate down to the aunt's house for a few nights while Theresa was out of town. Turns out, Theresa got back from her trip earlier than expected. And Michelle's there waiting in bed for John. She thought it was John walking in the room. Turns out it was Theresa."

"I can only imagine," Angela said, rolling her eyes. "Then Michelle and Theresa got into an actual physical fight?"

Alex said, "Michelle claims Theresa chased after her but tripped and tumbled down the stairs."

Angela said, "So what about the wine that spilled all over the walls and stairs?"

I said, "It was all part of the setup. Michelle admitted they tossed the wine all over the walls. It was easy enough to say Theresa had been drinking."

Angela sipped her drink. "I'm still shocked that Andy Meredith was willing to put his job on the line to help John."

"His wife said he was spending money left and right without telling her where the money was coming from. It took some time for her to put it all together, even though she knew all along he'd helped John. She never realized John paid him."

Angela said, "Isn't there a chance he was killed because of what he knew, about what really happened?"

"I thought about that," I said. "But the night he was killed, he wasn't supposed to be there. He took the call, by chance, and was shot point-blank when he walked through the door."

Angela got up from the chair and finished what was left of her drink, then handed me the glass.

"Have you spoken with Roy?" I said.

Angela nodded. "But we have a lot more to discuss together."

"He and his kid have a funny way of going about their business," I said, standing from my chair.

Angela stepped over to me and gave me a hug, pulling me close as she whispered into my ear, "Take care of Alex. The good ones like her are hard to find."

• • • ● •● • ● • • •

Thank you for reading *The Last Ride*. The series continues in *The Crystal Pelican*. You can learn more about it and the other books in the Henry Walsh series by visiting my website: www.GregoryPayette.com

If you'd like to read the Henry Walsh series prequel for free,
sign up for my newsletter by visiting:
GregoryPayette.com/crossroad

Also by Gregory Payette

Visit GregoryPayette.com for the complete catalog:

HENRY WALSH MYSTERIES

Dead at Third

The Last Ride

The Crystal Pelican

The Night the Music Died

Dead Men Don't Smile

Dead in the Creek

Dropped Dead

Dead Luck

JOE SHELDON SERIES

Play It Cool

Play It Again

Play It Down

U.S. MARSHAL CHARLIE HARLOW

Shake the Trees

Trackdown

JAKE HORN MYSTERIES

Murder at Morrissey Motel

STANDALONES

Biscayne Boogie

Tell Them I'm Dead

Drag the Man Down

Half Cocked

Danny Womack's .38

Made in the USA
Monee, IL
19 July 2024

62077664R00177